# Death across the Chesapeake

A Max and Allison Hurlock Roaring 20s Mystery

By John Reisinger

*A mysterious mansion on Maryland's Eastern Shore,
an impossible murder in a locked room,
and a deadly secret.*

Glyphworks Publishing
2016

# Death across the Chesapeake

ISBN 978-0-9838818-4-1

www.johnreisinger.com

Glyphworks Publishing, 2016

Photo Credit: Karen Ketterman

# Author's note

This, the sixth adventure in the Max Hurlock Roaring 20s Mysteries, takes place in 1926, and finds Max and Allison in a mood to reminisce. Their first case, Death of a Flapper, was in 1922, when they had been married for over a year, and some have wondered what they did before that point. Up until now, their back story has been given short shrift, and revealed only in hints buried in the dialogue. In Death across the Chesapeake, we find out another piece of their past and the strange way it affects a case in the present.

Although each Max and Allison mystery is a stand-alone, it is part of their history. Though Death of a Flapper is their first official, high-profile case, it was not their first brush with crime. Max, of course, solved a murder on his ship during his service in the Great War, an incident that has been referred to several times already in the stories. Between the war and Death of a Flapper, however, Max and Allison were drawn into a puzzling case close to home, a case that might not be a murder at all. If it is, it must be handled with discretion, because it involves some very important (and reclusive) people in St Michaels. This case, and the people involved become part of a new case in 1926. This is the story of those cases and how they intertwined.

# Characters

Max and Allison Hurlock

Chief Tom Vickers......................Easton Police Chief

Charles Leroux............................Easton murder victim

Glenn, Jacqueline Stilwell......... Owners of Casa Leone

Ned Gunther..... .......................Property manager

Grayson Dunlop........................Tax accountant

Marsha Tolley............................Real estate broker

Harold Santino...........................Client of Leroux

Marie Leroux.............................Leroux's ex wife

Nigel Smythe-Cunningham.......New York Art dealer

Iris Dalrymple............................St Michaels librarian

Violet McGuinn..........................Stilwell's maid

Will Purdum..............................Bridge Company

Chip Carswell............................Reporter

Al White....................................Reporter

Bob Avery.................................Reporter

## Chapter 1
## The transom

# 1926

Like mourners at a funeral, the small group of people stood in the hallway in front of the closed office door talking in hushed tones and shaking their heads.

"I'm telling you, it's not like Charles to disappear. He always stops by for coffee in the mornings."

"Right," said a woman, "and when he's out or his place isn't open, he always puts a closed sign on his door."

The concerned group was standing in the upstairs corridor of the Stilwell Building, next to the courthouse in Easton, on Maryland's Eastern Shore. A small sign next to the door read;

*Chesapeake Investments*

*Charles Leroux, Broker*

"Knock again. Maybe he's in the back."

Someone banged loudly on the closed door. The sound seemed to echo in the hallway, but there was no reply, and no sound from inside Chesapeake Investments.

"Charles! Are you in there?"

"The transom's open about halfway, so if he's in there he can hear us."

"I think something's wrong."

"No; it's probably nothing. We should wait a while. He'll show up and laugh at us for worrying."

"Still, it's really odd."

"Should we call somebody?"

"Wait a minute. It looks like someone already did. Here comes the police."

The heads turned to see a thin young patrolman appearing at the top of the stairwell. We walked towards the group with a look of curiosity on his face.

"It's Fred DeGrange. Morning Fred. Who called you?"

"Morning," Officer DeGrange answered. "I'm just doing a follow up. We got a call last night around nine. A passerby out walking his dog said he heard what sounded like gunshots from this building. We sent a man over and he found the place locked up, so we figured it was a backfire somewhere. Anyway, I thought I'd take another look this morning and see if anything might have been going on. So what's everybody doing here?"

"Well, we've just been wondering why Charles hasn't shown up. Tell you the truth, we're a mite concerned, especially now that we know about gunshots."

"This his space?"

"Right. Chesapeake Investments. He's been here for about four months now. He's here every day like clockwork. And any time he closes, he hangs out a closed sign. But today nobody's seen or heard any sign of him."

Officer DeGrange tried the door with a loud rattle. "Locked. And you say he's usually here by now?"

"Not usually; always."

"Well, if he is here, it seems he doesn't want company."

"You gonna bust the door down, officer?"

DeGrange pushed back his hat and scratched his head thoughtfully. "No sense breaking a perfectly good door if we're not sure there's anything wrong yet. Maybe he just had a family emergency or something."

"But he always has that closed sign out when he's not there. So if there is no sign, that means he should be there now."

"Or maybe he never went home last night!" said someone ominously.

Officer DeGrange squatted and looked through the keyhole. "Can't see anything. Looks like there's a key in the keyhole on the inside."

"Well, that proves he must be in there, doesn't it?" someone said.

"Is there another door to this space?" DeGrange asked.

"No. This is it. There's a window but it has bars because Charles handles money."

DeGrange frowned in thought, then looked up at the transom over the door. "Anybody have a stepladder?"

After some discussion, someone went back into an adjacent office and came back with a stepladder.

"Now who's the tallest?" said the DeGrange.

Grayson Dunlop, former star of the Easton High basketball team cautiously stepped up on the ladder and peeked over the edge of the transom. His eyes widened.

"Oh, jeez. Charles is in there, all right, but..."

"But what?"

"He's lying on the floor."

"*Now* we break it down," said the DeGrange. "Everybody stay back. I don't want anyone in the room unless I tell you."

DeGrange threw his weight against the door and it swung inward with a splintering crash. Inside was a neat office with a desk, several file cabinets, several overstuffed chairs, and a chalkboard on the wall covered with stock symbols and prices. In the center of the room, crumpled on a blue oriental rug, was Leroux lying on his back.

While the others clustered around the doorway for a better look, Officer DeGrange cautiously approached Charles Leroux.

"Mr. Leroux; are you all right? Mr. Leroux?"

In the doorway, a woman screamed. "Oh, my God; he's dead!"

DeGrange looked at the body and noticed three ugly bullet holes; two in the chest and one on the wrist with powder burns clearly visible. He squatted down and felt the wrist. There was no pulse, and the flesh was cold.

DeGrange looked around. There was no sign of a struggle and nothing seemed out of place. The door had clearly been locked from the inside, the sole window was barred, and the transom was too high and too small for anyone to exit that way. There was no gun in sight, so it wasn't a suicide, but who could have shot him, and how could he have done it? DeGrange shook his head.

"This kind of stuff just doesn't happen in the Stilwell Building. It just doesn't."

*John Reisinger*

## Chapter 2
## Looking back

In a small house 15 miles to the west, just past the town of St Michaels, Allison Hurlock stood in the doorway of the cozy upstairs room and critically surveyed its contents. There were two easy chairs, a table holding a battered notebook and a porcelain statue of a tiger, and several framed documents on the walls.

"So where do we start?" she said finally.

Her husband Max exhaled a long breath as he looked around the room. "Good question, but if we are going to have a baby in a few months, we have to have a room for him."

"Her," said Allison.

"...and it's either this trophy room or the spare bedroom, unless you want me to tackle an addition to the place," said Max.

"One addition is plenty, Max. Look, the trophy room was my idea in the first place; to have a room to display our mementoes from the crazy cases we were involved in. But now we have to make room and paint the walls pink."

"Blue."

"Anyway, most of the items aren't very big. We can put the stuff in the spare bedroom; maybe in a special corner."

"Yes," said Max. "That should do nicely until they can build a nice, tasteful Hurlock Museum."

Allison walked into the room and absently petted the tiger figurine. "So I repeat; where do we start? I don't want to just drag this all into the next room. We really need to make an inventory, or at least a list of what we have according to the case it came from. Then we can arrange it in a logical fashion; maybe even label the things. I have a pencil and paper here. Why don't I pull up a chair to that table and start with the list while you rummage through the loot."

"All right," said Max, picking up the old notebook on the table and thumbing through the dog-eared pages. "Here we have a piece of genuine Americana: a bootlegger's notebook of all his clients and liquor runs. It's a nice souvenir of our very first case together; that Taylor-Bradwell business in Moorestown, New Jersey back in 1922."

"The Taylor-Bradwell business?" said Allison, raising her eyebrows. "You make it sound as if you were selling soap. It was a double murder; the son of one of your old Navy buddies and his former fiancée found shot to death in her locked bedroom."

Max smiled. "A very interesting case, I have to admit. Normally, the police would assume a murder-suicide by a jilted ex fiancée, especially since the door was locked from the inside, but they were both shot several times in the head." *(Death of a Flapper)*

"And, as I recall, with a gun owned by Robert Bradwell's brother," Allison added. "Add a third murder, a Shakespeare-quoting widow, and a nervous part-time bootlegger, and you've got a real brain twister. Not to mention the fact that you almost made yourself the fourth victim."

Max blushed a little. "I think you were more sore at me than the killer was. Anyway, it ended well, and you got a good magazine article about flappers out of it."

Allison leaned back in the chair and smiled. "Yes; I enjoyed doing the research on the fast-paced world of the flapper. Of course, I'll bet you would have enjoyed it even more."

"As a purely academic exercise, of course," Max grinned.

Allison pointed to an ornate framed certificate hanging on the wall near the window.

"And then we have our honorary official lifetime membership in the otherwise exclusive Jekyll Island Club down in Georgia."

Max looked at the certificate. "I suppose we should be especially honored to be the only club members that are not millionaires. And it all started with a letter from a damsel in distress." *(Death on a Golden Isle)*

"It all started," Allison reminded him, "with a poisoning, and Eva Dawkins's fear of being arrested for her husband's murder. Of course, you found out that she wasn't nearly as dangerous as the predatory Miss Clarice Bailey."

"Now, now, Allison. I realize that you girls weren't the best of pals..."

"Somehow, I have trouble chumming up with a spoiled femme fatale while she was trying to steal my husband; it's a social skill I never mastered and don't intend to."

Max smiled. "Clarice Bailey wasn't nearly as irresistible as she thought she was...Say, here's a little exhibit I almost forgot; a menu from your old Roland Park hangout, Morgan Millard's, with a handwritten note on it from the great Houdini himself, right after he brought the house down at that séance by exposing the medium as a fraud."

Allison looked at the note. "Beware of assumptions and misdirection it says. I still can't figure out how he wrote that there and we never saw him do it."

"That's why they call it magic," said Max, "but it helped solve the case of the lighthouse keeper murdered in his lighthouse near Crisfield." (*Death the Lighthouse*)

"And it helped you save your two watermen friends from getting railroaded for the crime," added Allison. "I'm glad that awful Gaston Means got his comeuppance."

Max nodded and picked up a porcelain figurine from the table. "And here is our friend the blindfolded tiger statue from that case up in New York. (*Death and the Blind Tiger*) It's the only time we ever received a clue from a murder victim *before* he was killed."

"Creepy," was all Allison could say.

"You know this tiger should go with the mash note you received from Dorothy Parker on the same case," Max reminded her.

Allison smiled at the memory. "Just think; I was invited to the Algonquin round table by Dorothy Parker."

"Only after she tried to cut you down with that tongue of hers and you stood up to her."

"Yes. Country mouse indeed! Meanwhile, you were busy trying to solve a murder with more suspects than you could count. It would have been harder to find someone who *didn't* want to kill Mr. Connelly. Still, it was so exciting being in New York."

"More exciting than St Michaels?"

Allison gave him her "You have to be kidding" expression, and Max picked up another framed letter.

"For my money, this is the jewel of the collection," Max said, holding the frame high.

"Oh, yes;" Allison recalled, "the letter from Glenn Curtiss inviting you to Florida to catch the invisible man who was killing off Florida real estate developers." *(Death in Unlikely Places)*

"He's one of the giants of aviation, second only to the Wright Brothers....maybe,... and he needed my help."

Allison catalogued the letter. "Is that everything?"

"Well, there's an ashtray from the Casa Zorayda speakeasy in St Augustine...oh, and the magic beans you picked up in the Voodoo shop."

"The ones that were supposed to help me get pregnant."

"I suppose they worked," said Max, "although I think I helped."

Allison smiled.

"Ah," said Max, "here's a copy of American Show Dog Magazine with that article you wrote back in 1920. The only dog article you ever wrote as I recall."

Allison looked at the magazine and read the note pinned to the cover. "Good article, Allison. You covered Irish Wolfhounds almost as well as I do. Signed, Jacqueline Stilwell."

"Jacqueline Stilwell," Max repeated, shaking his head. "Now there was a character worthy of the Eastern Shore. I can still see her face when the police chief Vickers accused her of murdering her husband at their lavish mansion Casa Leone and my reporter pal Chip Carswell started digging up her yard looking for the body."

"Yes, and you got drawn into it as well," Allison said. "I'm glad that's over. Well, anything else?"

"A few odds and ends. We can put them in a box and stash it in the closet."

"This isn't so bad. We can arrange it in the guest bedroom. It'll be like sleeping in a family album." She folded the list and stretched. "What say we have a glass of lemonade to catch our breath?"


A few minutes later, Max and Allison were seated on wicker chairs on their porch with glasses of lemonade. The sun was getting higher and the cicadas were tuning up for the day. The surrounding woods were a mosaic of soft green with patches of sunlight scattered about.

Allison took a sip of her lemonade.

"How do you feel?" Max asked.

She shifted slightly in the chair. "Morning sickness doesn't usually start until the sixth week or so and its only been about four, but sometimes I wonder if there's a better way of doing this."

"You're doing fine," said Max, looking at the brightness on the horizon. "You'll be as good at motherhood as you are at everything else. All those souvenirs we just went through are yours as well as mine. We're a team, and a damned good one."

Allison took another sip and looked at the woods in silence for a while. Finally, she spoke. "We have been through a lot, haven't we?"

"Hey, I told you our life was going to be an adventure. You should have known it the first time we met."

Allison smiled. "Oh, yes. Most couples meet, court a bit, then get married for better or worse, but not us. We had to be different."

"Well, to be fair, it wasn't all by choice. There was a war, an epidemic, and a bunch of other complications..."

"Including a murder on a Navy ship and that weird business of the Irish Wolfhound at Casa Leone," Allison reminded him. "How we wound up married with all that going on is a mystery in itself."

"Maybe you should write *that* story someday," said Max. "That would liven up some of those magazines you write for."

"It would, but who would believe it? I hardly believe it all myself," said Allison.

"The whole thing was pretty unlikely. I was working at a repair garage on Route 1 to pay for college at

13

Maryland State in College Park, and you were a Goucher girl returning from research in Washington."

Allison nodded. "I remember it was raining in buckets, and I was on my way home from DC. I was low on gas and my tire was losing air, so I pulled into your garage. You came out in the pounding rain and asked if I wanted my windshield washed. It was the first laugh I had had all day. You filled my tank, fixed my tire, and came by to see me the next day with flowers."

"I told you; the flowers were for the car in case it didn't make it."

"Sure they were. We started seeing each other and you graduated and went off to join the Navy and fight the Kaiser. I graduated and went to work at the Sunpapers in Baltimore."

"But I finally got back."

"After solving a murder on your ship and palling around with that Collette in France. I was worried about that."

"Needlessly. Collette was someone I had to work with at the port of Brest to help with the repatriation once the Armistice was signed. She was a nice person who had a lot of tragedy in her life, including a husband killed in the war. France is full of Collettes."

"But you liked her."

"I liked her very much. She was intelligent, poised, and easy on the eyes, just like you. Most of all, she was not only a woman, but the only person I could talk to who wasn't in the Navy. That meant a lot at that point, but I was always anxious to get back to you."

"Then we got engaged and came over to the Eastern Shore and met some very interesting people. The best was your Uncle Bingo."

Max smiled. "Good old Uncle Bingo. The world's champion grouch...to everyone but you. He went off to California and left us the house as a wedding present."

"God bless him. So years later, here we are; several solved murder cases under our belt and ready to settle down to a life of domestic tranquility with our new baby."

"And I have gone from employee to independent consultant, so I can make my own schedule. That should come in handy when the baby comes."

"Yes. Do you think we'll ever get involved in another murder case?"

"Don't ask me. I didn't go looking for the cases we did get involved in. They showed up at our doorstep. Still, I think things have finally quieted down."

"Amen."

Max put his arm around her and pulled her closer, then frowned.

"Do you hear that?"

"Just a couple of ducks having a domestic dispute."

"I don't think so. It sounds like....a car coming."

"Well, tell them to go away. If it's a Prohibition agent, tell him we gave at the office."

"It's headed this way apparently."

Allison sat up. "Probably someone coming here just to break our mood."

A Model A appeared around a bend in the driveway.

"That's Chief Vickers from the Easton Police," said Max.

"And judging by his grim expression, he's not here to sell us tickets to the policeman's ball."

The car crunched to a stop on the crushed oyster shell driveway and a short grizzled man with a bushy mustache was out and up the steps to the front porch in one motion.

"Mornin' Max. Mornin' Miss Allison."

"What brings you down this way, Tom?" Max asked, getting right down to business.

Vickers wiped some perspiration from his forehead with the back of his sleeve. "I was in St Michaels just up the road seeing my sister. I called in to the office and they said there' s been a murder in Easton. Max I need your help. You too, Miss Allison."

"Sorry, Tom. I'm pretty busy. Besides, you've had murders in town before. You certainly don't need me."

"This one's different. Charles Leroux, a stockbroker, shot three times. They found him in a locked room."

Max nodded. "All right. You have my attention. It just got interesting."

"And it happened in the Stilwell Building."

Allison groaned. "Oh, no."

Max smiled. "Correction; it just got *very* interesting. But that doesn't explain why you need me."

"Come on Max. You're the detective. Figure it out. Glenn and Jacqueline Stilwell own the building and named it after themselves. They live in Casa Leone, the biggest, most mysterious and lavish mansion on the Eastern Shore, and have a staff of security guards all around. They are wealthy and eccentric and aren't shy about throwing their weight around. That means they draw attention. The Stilwells will be breathing down my neck to solve this case in their building before the tenants start to bail out. Jacqueline Stilwell has been sore at me since I accused her of murdering her husband and dug up half her yard to try to prove it back in 1920."

"Yes; that *was* a bit awkward," Max admitted.

"So what sort of cooperation am I going to get out of them? They'll be demanding action on one hand and hampering me on the other. But she tolerates you and actually likes Allison. I need you both as a buffer."

Max looked at Allison.

"I see the problem," she said. "Max, maybe we can help out."

Max sighed. "You know how I never really liked being a detective? Well I like being a buffer even less. But as usual, Allison's right. We should help you out."

"Thanks, both of you. I'm afraid we can't pay you, but..."

"Never mind that," said Max. "So why don't you head on back to Easton. Allison and I will drive up separately and we'll meet you at the Stilwell building in an hour. If anyone asks, we were passing by and were curious. Then we'll see how it goes."

The chief left, and a few minutes later, Max and Allison were in their Model A and heading towards Easton.

"So it looks like we'll have to tangle with the Stilwells again," said Max. "I knew they bought that office building up in Easton a few years back, but I never thought we'd get involved with them again."

"Our paths seem destined to cross," said Allison. "Why, even before we were married, people were buzzing about Casa Leone, that huge estate the Stilwells were building. Then the rumors started to fly about the mysterious rich folks from Pittsburgh and their strange ways."

"We got dragged into it even then," said Max. "Chief Vickers and Chip Carswell at the Star Democrat paper were determined to prove Jacqueline Stilwell had murdered her husband."

Allison chuckled. "I remember that whole episode, and you can bet Jacqueline Stilwell does, too. It all started before we were even married and were in the town library with Iris Dalrymple and the formidable Mrs. Stilwell blew in, complete with Irish Wolfhound in tow."

"I remember it, too. How could I forget? Too bad we couldn't put *that* in our trophy room!"

18

## Chapter 3
## Pieces of the past

# 1919-1920

On a bright spring day in 1919, Max Hurlock and his fiancée, Allison Winslow were in the midst of a whirlwind visit to the Eastern Shore, Max's old stomping grounds, and their future home. Passing through the town of St Michaels in a Model T Max borrowed from his uncle Bingo, they decided to drop by the library and see its know-it-all librarian, Iris Dalrymple. After the introductions, Max had a question.

"Say, Iris, do you know who that yellow Stutz Bearcat outside belongs to?"

St Michaels town librarian and all around authority on nearly everything, Iris Dalrymple looked up from a book she was showing Allison.

"Oh, that's Mrs. Stilwell. She lives in that new mansion they're building over in the Bellvue-Ferry Neck area. She emerges from the place occasionally and drives into town; usually at excessive speed. She browses through the shops but never buys anything."

Max looked out the window. "I suppose that's her, now."

Coming down the street was a tall, thin woman in an expensive suit, and with a fox fur around her shoulders and a huge Irish Wolfhound on a leash.

19

"I doubt that she's in town to apply for a job at the packing house," Max remarked.

"I think she's coming in here," said Allison.

The door opened and Mrs. Stilwell appeared. With her was an invisible cloud of some no doubt expensive perfume and a very large Irish Wolfhound. "Good morning. May I bring my dog in here?"

Iris Dalrymple shrugged. "As long as he's housebroken and doesn't eat any of the books."

"...or the patrons," Allison murmured. She wasn't sure if the huge animal was a dog or a pony in a dog costume.

"Is this the local library?" Mrs. Stilwell asked.

"This is it," said Iris. "I'm Iris Dalrymple and this is Max Hurlock and his lovely fiancée Allison Winslow."

"Jacqueline Stilwell. How do you do? Is this the entire library?"

"I usually tell people that this is just a branch. Our main library is on Fifth Avenue in New York City."

Mrs. Stilwell smiled. "I see; very amusing. Well, I'm just getting acquainted with the town...such as it is."

"You live in that big new mansion over towards Bellvue, don't you?" said Iris.

"The proper name is Casa Leone," the woman said coldly.

"*Quel est le nom de votre chien*?" said Max.

"Hercules," she answered, then caught herself. "Wait. How did you know I spoke French?" she demanded of Max.

"You have a slight accent," said Max, smiling genially. "It sounded too slight to be a native one, more likely to be the accent of someone who only spent a few years in France. I'm guessing you went to school there, something not unusual for someone who lives in a mansion...whatever its name."

Mrs. Stilwell looked at Allison. Allison nodded agreement. "*C'est vrai.*"

A storm seemed to be brewing on Mrs. Stilwell's brow, but Allison defused the situation by petting the dog. "Hercules, you are beautiful. I covered dog shows for the Baltimore Sun and you would have won any of them." Hercules appreciated the attention and responded by trying to lick Allison's face, a move that Mrs. Stilwell quickly checked with a pull on the leash.

Mrs. Stilwell looked at the three. "You have a good eye for dogs, Miss Winslow. I myself write occasional pieces for the dog periodicals. As for the rest, well, I suppose a little curiosity is to be expected, but my husband and I value our privacy. Please respect that. Good day."

"Good move, Allison," said Max.

"Yes," said Iris Dalrymple. "I was afraid we were going to be unwilling participants in a revival of The Hound of the Baskervilles."

"How about the husband?" Allison asked. "Have you ever seen him?"

She nodded. "Once or twice. He comes into town occasionally, but mostly people see him in his yacht; a big black sailboat named 'Centurion'. Some folks say he sleeps there sometimes. He's big guy who wears a patch over one eye, like a pirate. Some say it's from a duel. I'm telling you, the Mad Stilwells are the talk of the shore these days."

As they emerged back on the street, Max and Allison saw the yellow Stutz Bearcat roaring off in a crunch of oyster shells. Hercules sat in the passenger seat looking almost as tall as his mistress.

"So these are the stout yeomanry of St Michaels," Allison remarked as they watched the car disappear down the road. "These are the kind of people for whom the word 'quirky' was invented. Still, I have to admit, they're sort of endearing in an unhinged sort of a way."

"Salt of the earth," said Max. "But now you know why I was considered the dull one around here."

When Max and Allison's wedding day in Baltimore finally arrived, the weather was perfect and everyone got along, at least outwardly. In his rented tuxedo, Max couldn't stop grinning, while Allison easily outshone every other woman present. Max's mother cried from happiness while Allison's mother cried with relief that all her planning came out so well. Star-Democrat reporter Chip Carswell was the best man. Various citizens of both Roland Park and St Michaels attended.

At the reception, the Eastern Shore guests were in awe of the plush surroundings of the Belvedere Hotel in Baltimore. The band played some of the new jazz numbers along with more traditional music and everyone was having a good time.

Chip Carswell put his glass on a nearby table and lit a cigarette. "Max, you hear the latest about Casa Leone?"

"Not Casa Leone again," Max groaned. "So what happened? Did one of Jacqueline Stilwell's mutts get loose and dig up someone's garden?"

"Better than that, Max. It seems that Glenn Stilwell has disappeared! Rumor has it that he's been murdered. He sailed off in his boat, the Centurion, and no one has seen him or the boat since."

"Has Mrs. Stilwell reported her husband missing?"

"No, but some of the workers there said the Stilwells used to fight like the Kilkenny Cats. Maybe she did him in."

Max gave Chip a pained expression.

"All right, Max. Be skeptical, but you have to admit it sounds strange."

"Everything about that place sounds strange," said Max, "but there's a big distance between strange and murder."

Carswell took a sip of punch. "Maybe not as far as you think."


That night, the newlyweds took the train to Philadelphia and the Bellvue Statford Hotel for a short honeymoon. Since they were going to live on the Eastern Shore, they thought a city would be a nice change. Some months afterwards, Max and Allison had settled in their new home near St Michaels on the Eastern Shore. Combining business with pleasure, Allison had written two articles about Philadelphia after their honeymoon and sold one to a travel magazine. Max was working on various construction projects for an engineering firm out of his office in Easton and shopping for airplanes in his spare time. He was fascinated by flying and wanted to try a war surplus Curtiss Jenny.


"Mornin' Miz Allison." Frosty Fred, the local iceman tipped his hat as he pulled up in his ice truck a few weeks later. Allison was seated on the porch with her typewriter on a small table in front of her.

"So, maybe 50 pounds today? It's been pretty hot," said Fred, wiping his brow.

"Fifty pounds would be fine," she said. Let me get the money."

Fred got the ice tongs and lifted a block of ice, then took it in the house. He reappeared in a few seconds.

"That's a pretty old icebox," he remarked.

"Uncle Bingo left it," said Allison. "I would have gotten one of those new refrigerators. Oh...sorry. I guess that's a sore subject."

Fred shrugged. "That's the way it is, I guess. Folks get electricity and pretty soon they want all these new appliances. Sooner or later, I'll be out of business."

Allison suddenly smelled a possible article in the making. "I suppose most of your customers are the older places. Anyone building a new house would get the latest appliances."

"Yeah, that's a fact, but now that you mention it, I got a big ice order just a week ago from Casa Leone."

"Really? I wouldn't have thought they'd have an icebox."

"That was what made it so peculiar," said Fred. "Near as I could see, they don't. I brought two hundred pound blocks into the kitchen...biggest dang kitchen you ever seen...and saw two good sized, brand new refrigerators. They told me to put the ice on the counter, then they cover the blocks with blankets."

"That does sound odd," said Allison.

"Well, they paid up, so I can't complain," said Fred. He paused. "Say, do you hear that noise?"

Allison had heard the noise, a far off droning sound, like a motor boat at full speed.

"It's getting louder," she said.

"Where's it coming from?"

The sound was much louder now, and seemed to fill the air, but there was no sign of what was making it. Finally, a biplane roared past just a few hundred feet overhead, shaking the leaves on the trees.

"Dang!" said Fred. "An airplane. Don't see many of them around here."

"Well, you will," said Allison. "That's my husband Max with his Curtiss Jenny."

The airplane circled and dropped down to a somewhat bumpy landing. The plane taxied up to the barn and stopped. The sudden silence was total.

A man Allison didn't know lifted himself out of the pilot's cockpit while Max bounded out of the forward cockpit and ran up to Allison and embraced her.

"Here it is, Allison. Isn't it beautiful? One genuine war surplus Curtiss Jenny. And it's all ours."

The pilot, who Max introduced as Bill Otto appeared, wiping his hands on a rag. "She's looking good, Max; smooth as a baby's belly. You'll be soloing in no time."

"Bill is teaching me to fly," Max added, somewhat unnecessarily.

Allison walked over to the airplane. It was a maze of wire bracing and wings, almost like a giant kite. The engine made odd tapping and popping sounds as it cooled, making the contraption seem almost alive.

"I can't wait to get you up there," Max continued. "Allison, I'm telling you, there is nothing like it. You'll love flying."

Allison tentatively poked the wing fabric with her finger. "I'm sure I will, Max. It's the part about crashing to the ground I'm not so crazy about."

Later, when Bill Otto had taken the airplane back to a farm near Easton where he lived, Max and Allison sat on the porch with watching the lengthening shadows in the trees, Max was still going strong.

"You will love the view from up there," he said. "We even flew over Casa Leone. It's quite a place."

"So I've heard. It's the talk of the town." She told Max about the strange ice delivery Frozen Fred had told her about. Max looked interested.

"Hmmm. I suppose there's a simple explanation, but still..."

"What?"

"Well, when we were flying over Casa Leone a while ago, I noticed something strange." Max leaned back in the chair thoughtfully. "Over in one corner near the fence, was an area of freshly turned earth. It was very noticeable, even from the air."

Allison shrugged. "So maybe they have a garden. Even rich people have gardens sometimes."

Max chuckled. "Allison, you met Jacqueline Stilwell. Did she strike you as the farming type?"

"Point taken, but maybe one of the cooks is raising vegetables."

"I don't think so," said Max. "The area is too small, maybe four by eight feet."

Allison looked shocked. "Max, that's the size..."

"...of a gravesite. I know."


For the next few weeks, Max took the airplane up solo several times and finally brought it home for good. Now that he could solo, he prodded Allison to go with him. After resisting, Allison finally agreed.

"Great!" Max exclaimed. He produced a brown leather flying hat, complete with goggles. "This is for you."

Allison examined it. "Well, this is nice. Not only do I get to risk my life, but I have to look silly while I'm doing it."

"Now, Allison, just give it a try. You'll like it, I promise."

Allison climbed unsteadily up to the front passenger cockpit. "The last time I heard that phrase was when my mother was trying to get me to eat liver and onions."

"And?"

"I didn't like it."

With a roar, the Jenny lifted off the ground and soared over the nearby farms and water. Max leveled out as they passed over St Michaels. He picked up the speaking tube to talk to Allison in the front cockpit.

"How do you like that view? We can go back if you'd like."

"Max, where has this been all my life? This is wonderful! Don't you dare go back yet."

"I thought you were terrified. What happened?"

"I opened my eyes...in more ways than one. Hey, Max; let's fly over Casa Leone. Maybe we can buzz Mrs. Stilwell"

"Tally ho. We're on our way." Max banked right and headed south.

"Look at the water below," said Allison, clearly still excited. "It's beautiful. Max; this is like being flying gypsies!"

"Hey; why don't we name the airplane Gypsy?" said Max.

"Gypsy it is," said Allison. "Hey, I see the mansion. It looks huge."

Casa Leone was more like a Spanish or Italian villa than a mansion. It had red tile roofs and a three story tower in the center.

"Impressive," said Allison. "So where's the patch of freshly dug earth you found a couple of weeks ago?"

"Over by the fence to the left. Say, that's strange."

"What's strange?"

"I can barely make out the area now. They must have planted grass on it."

"That doesn't sound like a garden, Max."

Max frowned in thought. "No, it sure doesn't. I think I'll give Chip Carswell a call when we get back."


At the offices of the Easton Star–Democrat, Chip Carswell's eyes widened.

"A freshly dug grave? .. and blocks of ice? I knew it. Jacqueline Stilwell did away with her husband and buried him in the backyard. Max is the greatest story of my career."

"Now wait a minute, Chip," said Max, holding up a hand like a cop stopping traffic, "I never said it was a grave, just some unexplained disturbed dirt."

"Then how do you explain the ice, Max?"

"How would I know? Maybe their electric refrigerator broke down."

"And with their money, they couldn't afford to get it fixed? That's banana oil, Max. Here's the way I see it. Jacqueline Stilwell bumped off her husband Glenn. Then she finds she has a body on her hands and she comes up with a plan. She has to stash the body until she has a chance to dig the grave. Maybe she has a loyal servant do it, or maybe her property manager. Either way, she has to keep the body from decomposing while she's arranging everything, so she orders up the ice."

"Chip, for Pete's sake...."

'Then she takes out that black sailboat of his, or maybe she gets someone else to do it, and sinks it over in deeper water. Then she takes the dingy and returns to Casa Leone. Then, when she's ready, she buries the body in the fresh grave and plants grass over it. The perfect crime."

Max shook his head. "Look, Chip; if she did kill her husband, why would she have to preserve the body? She could bury it the same night. Why wait around?"

Chip stopped with his mouth half open. "Why wait?"

"The ice was delivered a week ago. The boat disappeared just before that."

Chip nodded. "Right, so by the time the ice was delivered, he'd been dead for a couple of days. That fits my theory."

"Sure," said Max, "and I saw the dug up area just about the time the ice was delivered."

"So?"

"So, if the boat was gone, and Glenn Stilwell was dead, and the grave was dug, what was the ice for?"

"I told you, Max; to preserve the body."

"For what?" said Max. "Why not just bury him? Maybe wait until dark, but that was it. Why wait beyond that?"

Chip exhaled heavily. "All right. I don't know why she waited. All I know is she did. You'll see, Max. This will be the scoop of a lifetime. I'm talking to Chief Vickers tomorrow. Casa Leone is in his area."

"Look, Chip," said Max. "Let me see what I can find out. The police could never get a warrant based on that information. Just give me a week or so."


That night, Allison took a stab at fried chicken. Max said it wasn't bad, at least the parts she was able to pry from the pan. The boiled vegetables were better and the Eastern Shore was overrun by fresh tomatoes, so the meal was a good one overall, and conducive to deep conversation. They talked of the thrill of flying and where Gypsy might take them next. Then the talk turned to Allison's literary efforts.

"Dogs?" said Max. "Why would you want to write about dogs?"

"Are you kidding? The world is crawling with dog-lovers. They'd love an in-depth look at man's best friend; especially all the talk about the best retrievers you hear around here. Then, of course, you have people who have the more exotic breeds, like Mrs. Stilwell and that big galoot Hercules we saw a while ago."

"Well, one thing should help you; dog lovers are always ready to bend your ear about the wonders of their pooch."

Max suddenly stopped.

"Uh oh," said Allison, "I know that look. That's your I-just-thought-of-something look. I'm surprised you don't have a light bulb suspended over your head."

"Allison," said Max, slowly. "Have you considered interviewing Jacqueline Stilwell?"

31

"She'd never go along with that. Remember that stuff about privacy?"

"True," said Max, "but she seemed to soften somewhat when you asked about the dog. Maybe she'd be more open than you think."

"Maybe." Allison still seemed uncertain. "Of course, I can't sit on Main Street everyday waiting for her to show up again."

"Oh, no," said Max., "You can just drop in on her at home."

"What? You want me to storm Casa Leone single handedly?"

"Look. They have a gatehouse. You can just drive up and tell them you met Mrs. Stilwell in St Michaels and would like her input on Irish Wolfhounds for an article you're writing on dogs of the Eastern Shore."

Allison nodded slowly. "You know, there's a chance she might bite on that sort of bait. It's worth a try. I'll head on out here tomorrow. Thanks, Max."

Max smiled. "Always willing to help. Oh, by the way; while you're there, you might want to see if you can see or hear anything about Glenn Stilwell's disappearance."

Allison started. "So that's why you have this sudden fascination with my interview selection. You want me to snoop around for you and your pal Chip Carswell to see if there's any scandal to write about."

"Well, if it wouldn't be too much trouble..."

Allison was nodding as she warmed to the idea. "Yes. That might just work at that. Very well. I'll get in that castle and then you just watch my smoke. I'll find out what happened to Glenn Stilwell. You're not the only detective around Chez Hurlock. This is exciting. I can't wait for tomorrow."

Max grasped her hand. "That's my Allison. You know, they say you can make tomorrow come faster if you go to bed early."

She stood up and arched her eyebrows.

"I thought you'd never ask."

*John Reisinger*

# Chapter 4
## Casa Leone

The next morning, Allison dropped Max off at his office in Easton, then drove down to Bellvue and found the road to Casa Leone. The drive was peaceful and scenic, with quiet, tree-lined country roads over flat terrain. Everything was so bucolic, Allison found herself singing *"Ain't we got fun?"* as she drove along. To her surprise, the man at the gatehouse, after a phone call to the main house, let her through.

Allison had to work to keep from constantly saying "Wow!" as she approached the main house over immaculately landscaped grounds that resembled nothing so much as an English manor. The guard had opened an inner gate to allow her inside and she was aware of a vague feeling of being trapped.

From flying over the property with Max earlier, Allison recognized much of the layout, including a huge and somewhat sinister-looking outbuilding that was obviously a kennel for who knew how many dogs. The place was not made to welcome visitors, Allison thought.

The main house grew bigger as she approached until it threatened to crowd out everything else. A square central tower looked down menacingly on a stone walled patio. On the patio, seated at an ornate iron table and sipping a

35

drink was Jacqueline Stilwell, wearing a light blue summer dress and weighed down with at least several pounds of jewelry. Next to her sat the hulking form of Hercules, and he looked hungry.

Allison could smell the cloud of perfume that surrounded Mrs. Stilwell the moment she got out of the Model T. As she approached, Jacqueline Stilwell watched her.

"Good morning, Mrs...."

"I will give you five minutes. If what you have to say does not interest me, you will be escorted off the property," Mrs. Stilwell interrupted.

"Why, Mrs. Stilwell," said Allison, leaning slightly to pet Hercules. "I am here to talk about Irish Wolfhounds. How could that possibly fail to be interesting?"

Allison detected a faint smile. So far, so good.

"Thank you for seeing me, Mrs. Stilwell. I just knew that no article on dogs would be complete without your input on Irish Wolfhounds. I'm grateful your schedule would permit it."

She shrugged. "My schedule, as you put it, has become more flexible ever since...well, never mind."

Since you killed your husband? Allison thought.

They talked about Irish Wolfhounds for over an hour. It was a subject that obviously held a fascination for Mrs. Stilwell that outweighed her usual hostility to visitors.

"Now, Allison, you will notice certain aspects of a Wolfhound's coat. Hercules here...Ah; hello, Ned."

Allison looked around and saw a man approaching. He looked concerned.

"Jacqueline, you didn't tell me you had approved a visitor today," he said warily.

"It was a spur of the moment decision, Ned. She's writing a magazine article about Wolfhounds; how could I resist? Allison, this is Ned Gunther, our estate manager."

"And head of security," he reminded her.

"Oh, Ned; have you attended to that matter we discussed?"

Allison noticed that Ned's eyebrows went up. "Almost. There were some...problems we need to discuss..." He looked at Allison. "...in private."

"Now?"

"I'm afraid so. That thing we thought was settled might not be."

Mrs. Stilwell stood up abruptly, apparently highly agitated. "I think you have enough for your article Mrs. Allison. Good day. You know the way out."

As Allison beat a hasty retreat, she could hear Mrs. Stilwell speaking anxiously to Ned Gunther.

"I thought you were going to get rid of him once and for all!"

"Just a little longer," Gunther replied. "There were some unexpected problems."

Allison was glad to leave the gatehouse and Casa Leone behind her. She did not sing on the way home.

Max, meanwhile, was doing some digging of his own. From asking around, he found out that several of the staff at Casa Leone came into Easton every week for various supplies. Someone was due that day at Boswell's General Store. Max talked with Frank Boswell and got some information about the sort of gossip he might have heard, but nothing was conclusive.

"One strange thing;" said Boswell, "last time Stilwell's man came by for supplies, he bought a new shovel. He said the old one broke from too much digging. Says he asked that Ned Gunther fellow about it and he said he was digging a grave for Mrs. Stilwell's first love."

"A grave?" said Max. "Was he serious?"

"Nah. I guess he was kidding. Very funny, huh?"

"Hilarious," said Max.


That night, Max and Allison compared notes over some slightly burned pork chops.

"The grave was for Mrs. Stilwell's first love?" Allison exclaimed. "That settles it; she did him in for sure. Max, you have to tell Chief Vickers right away. She can't get away with this!"

"Now wait a minute," said Max, holding up his hands. "Before you go putting handcuffs on this woman, we need to step back a little. All we have are some coincidences and some overheard conversations that could mean any number of things. There is no real evidence."

"There's a body buried in the yard! What do you call that?"

"I call that conjecture. We have no idea what, if anything is in that yard, and without a search warrant, no one can find out."

"Well, then..."

"Allison, I appreciate your enthusiasm, but no court would issue a search warrant based on what we have. Besides..."

"Besides what?"

"Besides, I'm not convinced anything has happened to Mr. Stilwell. He could come sailing back any day now. I don't want to see everyone get worked up for nothing."

Allison started to object, then slumped down slightly in her chair. "Darn it, Max. You're right. We need more. We need something clear cut."

The next morning, Max called Chip Carswell to discuss Casa Leone. Chip was excited about what Max and Allison had learned, but Max settled him down,

"I guess you're right, Max," Carswell said. "We need a lot more evidence for a search warrant. I have a contact that might help. He's a waterman who lives in a small place just north of the Stilwell property. It seems the Stilwells, Mrs. Stilwell in particular, have been pressuring him to sell his place and move out. It looks like they want to own the entire island if they can."

"Well, that's one way to get privacy," Max observed.

"Anyway, my contact claims that the Stilwells' agents have been making veiled threats. One of them said something about threats to the Stilwells and how they needed the security. They said it could be dangerous for anyone living close by."

"Not very neighborly," said Max.

"But there's even more," said Carswell. "I have a contact at the Clerk's office. It seems the Glenn Stilwell filed a new will at the courthouse just three days before he disappeared. It leaves everything to Jacqueline. There's your motive."

"Hmmm," said Max. "I'm not sure how damning that is. As far as I could tell, Jacqueline pretty much has free access to all the money now."

"Scoff all you like, Max, but I'm going to talk to Chief Vickers and see if we have enough for a search warrant."

"Chip, wait a minute. This is all circumstantial. There's a basic flaw; how would Jacqueline pull all this off in full view of the staff? I mean, the place has gardeners, dog keepers, and I'm sure, several cooks and chambermaids swarming about the compound. They're practically bumping into each other. You couldn't sneeze in that place without someone knowing it, but you think she committed a murder under their noses? She couldn't take a chance that someone would see something and blab. It doesn't make sense. Besides we still don't know why anyone would wait several days to bury the body."

"I told you why; to make sure there was a dark night. That's why she needed the ice. I'll talk to you later."

Max hung up the phone and shook his head. "Everybody's a detective."

The phone rang the next morning while Max was getting ready to leave.

"Max; this is Chip at the paper. Have I got news for you!"

"Isn't that your job?" said Max, dryly.

"None of your cold water today, my friend. Today I will stand triumphant. Chief Vickers has obtained a search warrant for Casa Leone, and it includes digging up the grave where Jacqueline Stilwell buried her husband. Let's see you explain that away, Mr. Sherlock Hurlock."

"He's going out there today?"

"At eleven o'clock. I'm going with him and you're invited. That way, you'll be handy when I say I told you so."

"Look, Chip; I know we kid around, but this is serious. Listen carefully. There has been no murder. You're going to intrude on someone's privacy and look foolish. Chief Vickers is a great guy, but he's used to handling drunks and the occasional burglary in town. He's out of his depth here. He's going to be embarrassed and he's going to blame you."

"Max," said Chip in a more-in- sorrow-than-in-anger voice, "I never thought you would be the type to envy a pal. Why can't you just admit I was right?"

"You are not right. I'm trying to save you from destroying your career, and making an enemy of the police. Please; for once listen to me. Don't do it!"

"Look, Max. It's as plain as can be. The Stilwells have a fight; Glenn Stilwell disappears, along with the boat; Jacqueline has a grave dug and ice delivered; a day or two later, the grave gets covered over and grass is growing on top; the fella at the store tells you the manager broke a shovel digging a grave; Allison overhears Jacqueline Stilwell tell her manager to get rid of the body. That means they are going to move the body somewhere permanently once things settle down. That's why we have to act now. Why, it all fits together like a mystery story."

"Mystery stories are fictional," said Max. "What I'm telling you is..."

"Eleven o'clock, Max. If you want to go, be at the Stilwell's main gate. Otherwise, you can read about it in tomorrow's Star-Democrat."

The phone line went dead.

Max slumped in a chair and sighed. "That's what I'm afraid of."

Allison came into the room brushing her hair.

"I heard you on the telephone. What's all the drama? Not Casa Leone again?"

"I'm afraid so. The police chief has a search warrant and he's going out there with Chip to dig up the body and bring Mrs. Stilwell to justice at 11 today."

"Yikes. That should stir the pot a bit. Are you going, too?"

"Why should I?" Max said in an irritated tone. "I tried to talk him out of it, but he wouldn't listen. He's blinded by his desire for a big story. It's going to be an embarrassment, if not a disaster. I should wash my hands of the whole thing."

Allison raised her eyebrows. "But you're going anyway."

"What makes you say that?"

"Max, I know you pretty well by now. You're a fixer. You're one of the good guys. You're not going to stand by and let your friends walk into the lion's den alone. You'll go because, even if it makes you look bad, you want to be there to help if things start to come unglued."

"You're right," Max sighed. "I'm going. Maybe I can help soften the backlash when everything falls apart."

"You think it will?"

Max shook his head. "Allison, I don't know what's in that dug-up area, but I'll bet it isn't Glenn Stilwell."


Leaving Allison to put the finishing touches on her article about dogs and dog owners, Max got in the Model T and started towards Easton, where he intercepted Chip Carswell just before he left. Chip was surprised, but offered to take Max so there wouldn't be so many automobiles descending on Casa Leone at once. They didn't talk very much on the way. Chip was anxious and Max was resigned. All Chip would say was "You'll see, Max."

The guards at the gate to Casa Leone were surprised, but opened the gate when they saw the warrant brandished by Chief Vickers and his sergeant. They went inside the compound and saw the massive house looming ahead, seeming to glow slightly in the midday sun.

"This is some spread," said Chip. "I feel like I'm in Europe. And look at that place! I expect to see a bunch of Spanish noblemen come out on horseback."

"There's the dug up area," said Max.

Chip nodded. "A nice spot for a burial. You can see the river from there."

By the front terrace, Mrs. Stilwell was waiting for them with daggers in her eyes.

43

"Would you mind telling me why you saw fit to invade my home, and to bring these men?"

Chief Vickers introduced himself and handed her the search warrant. She read it and snapped her head up again.

"A search warrant? Of all the damned foolishness. And who are these other men? Surely they are not all police."

"No ma'am. This is Mr. Carswell. He volunteered to help with the digging, and this is Mr. Hurlock..."

"Oh, yes," said Mrs. Stilwell. "I remember Mr. Hurlock. I suppose your wife was here the other day just to spy on me."

"No, Mrs. Stilwell," said Max. "What she told you was true. She is writing an article and she did want your opinion. She said you were very informed and helpful."

Mrs. Stilwell was unappeased. "Then why are you here, Mr. Hurlock? Curiosity? There seems to be an abundance of it around here."

"Well, Mrs. Stilwell," said Max. "I feel responsible for all this. You see, I mentioned the dug up area I saw from an airplane and that started the ball rolling. One thing led to another and, well, here we are. The police have to follow through on these things. I do apologize for the intrusion. I hope we can clear things up."

"Humph. Well, Chief Vickers is it? What do you intend to do; frisk me? You'd better get started. I'd hate to take you away from chasing bootleggers a minute longer than necessary."

"Yes, ma'am. Sergeant, Chip; will you start to dig up that area over by the fence?"

The sergeant and Chip Carswell took shovels from the car and started towards the area in question."

"You will NOT dig up that area, you officious flatfoot!" Mrs. Stilwell was in full outrage mode. "I won't have it. I absolutely forbid it! You have no right!"

"We have a warrant, Mrs. Stilwell. I'm afraid we have to," said Vickers.

"Just what do you expect to find, the crown jewels or something?"

"No, ma'am. Your husband."

"Glenn? What would Glenn be doing in a hole in the ground? Why would...oh, my stars. Are you saying I killed Glenn?"

"What's going on here?" The manager, Mr. Gunther came running up, starting the arguments all over again. Chip Carswell and the sergeant, meanwhile, had already started digging.

"Now, Mrs. Stilwell," said Max. "I don't think this will take long and they'll be careful not to make a mess."

"They've already made a mess of Mrs. Stilwell's privacy!" Gunther joined the fray. "Look at them; they're down a foot already and throwing dirt everywhere."

"Mr. Hurlock says he's responsible for this," said Mrs. Stilwell. "He started it."

"I am sorry for the intrusion," said Max, "but it won't take long and maybe we can clear this up."

Mrs. Stilwell turned on Chief Vickers. "Now, back to my question. Exactly what do you think I've done? I have a right to know."

Chief Vickers cleared his throat as Chip Carswell and the sergeant continued to methodically dig in the background. "Mrs. Stilwell, we have reason to suspect that you murdered your husband and buried him there where they are digging after preserving the body for several days with ice to await a cloudy night so you wouldn't be seen."

"What? That's ridiculous. Of all the..."

"So then where is Mr. Stilwell, Ma'am?"

"He's on his boat somewhere, and no, I don't know when he'll be back."

"I can't believe this," Gunther began. "Mrs. Stilwell is a law abiding woman. This is an outrage. You should..."

"Chief?" came the voice of the sergeant, who stood with his shovel in his hand.

"Yes, sergeant?"

"We found something. It looks like a coffin."

"What?" Max was the only one who was surprised. Chief Vickers gave Mrs. Stilwell a meaningful glance and went to the excavation. The wooden lid of a coffin-like box was partially exposed in the loose earth.

"Clear the dirt off of it and let's have a look."

Chip and the sergeant cleared the dirt off on the top of the wooden box and began to pry at the lid.

"Chief, this is outrageous!" Mrs. Stilwell protested. "That is private property. That is..."

"I'm sorry, Ma'am," said the chief. "It's a little late for that. Now please stand back. We're going to see what's inside."

The chief motioned to Chip and the sergeant, who pulled the lid off the coffin. A circle of faces around the hole leaned in to look.

"What the...?" said Chief Vickers.

"That looks like...."

"A dog?" said Chip. "It's a dog!"

All heads turned towards Mrs. Stilwell. "How very observant," she said. "You are all great detectives. You can tell the difference between a man and a dog. That is Casey, my oldest and most loved Irish Wolfhound. Ned here calls him the love of my life. He died about a week ago and we laid him to rest. Of course we never dreamed that the local constabulary would turn out to be grave-robbers. Now, if the interests of justice have been served, I'll thank you to close the lid and let poor Casey rest in peace."

Carswell recovered first. "All right. So Glenn Stilwell isn't here. It just means he's somewhere else. He could be underneath this box just to throw us off. He could be..."

"Chip!" Max's voice brought him up short. He looked at Max. Max didn't speak. He just pointed toward the river. All heads turned.

Approaching the dock was a large , black sailboat.

Chip Carswell looked as if he was going to be sick. As if by a signal, he and the sergeant started frantically reburying the box.

Mrs. Stilwell turned to Chief Vickers. "You asked about my husband's whereabouts? I believe even you could locate him now."

Vickers stammered. "But, but what about the ice you had delivered when you have an electric icebox?"

Gunther chimed in. "Mrs. Vickers had an old friend from Washington here for dinner and wanted to do something special. She asked the cook to make an ice sculpture for the occasion. Any other questions?"

Chip was not quite ready to give up. "But who did you tell Mr. Gunther to get rid of a couple of days ago?"

"One of the watermen who has an adjoining property," said Gunther. "Mrs. Stilwell wants to buy his land and he's holding out for more money."

"Mr. Hurlock," said Mrs. Stilwell standing with her arms folded. "I suppose I have you to blame for this fiasco?"

Max gave what he hoped was a disarming smile. "It was a mix up; just some circumstantial evidence that pointed the wrong way. I'm very sorry."

She looked at him critically. "I'd say your judgment, not to mention your friends, leave a lot to be desired, Mr. Hurlock."

"Well..."

"Incredibly enough, however, I found your wife to be interesting, intelligent, and charming, so for her sake, I will forget this ridiculous scene and your apparent role in it...providing you get your friend and these Keystone Cops off of my property and keep them off. Oh, and I'd advise you all to be out of here before my husband gets the Centurion tied up and finds out about this. He's not as understanding as I am."

They all muttered apologies and beat a hasty retreat. Max restrained himself until they were past the front gate, then burst out laughing.

"Well," said Carswell, "I knew somebody would wind up saying I told you so, but I never thought it would be you. Look, Max. I really appreciate how you took the heat off of the chief and me. We could have both been fired if she'd decided to make a stink."

"That's what I figured. Not to mention making an enemy of the richest couple in the county. Well, no harm done, I guess."

That night, Max and Allison sat on the porch and watched the sun go down through the trees. Max sighed contentedly as Allison's specialty, macaroni with ketchup settled in his stomach.

"I can't believe it," said Allison. "Mrs. Stilwell didn't do her husband in after all. I feel strangely disappointed. How did you know?"

Max shrugged. "I didn't know everything of course. I had no idea what the hole was for, or the ice, but the theory that she would be able to kill and bury anyone in that complex without setting tongues wagging seemed unlikely. I also didn't buy the idea of using ice on the body. That would mean leaving it lying around for days, giving prying eyes more chances to see it. It just didn't add up."

"Well, maybe it takes a detective to know when there isn't a crime to solve."

Max made a dismissive gesture. "I am not a detective and have no desire to become one. I just keep noticing the loose ends of life and trying to tie them back together again, but sometimes you just can't. Today just clinches it. Anyway, at least you seem to have made a good impression on Mrs. Stilwell."

"Of course I did. I listened to her gas on about Irish Wolfhounds for almost an hour."

"Let's just hope the Stilwells don't carry grudges."

A tinny ring came from inside the house. "I'll get it," said Allison, rising from her chair. "Maybe it's my old editor begging me to come back to the Sunpapers."

Max brooded silently for a few minutes, staring out at the trees.

A minute later, Allison reappeared and flopped down on a wicker porch chair that squeaked in protest.

"Well, we have a dinner invitation for two weeks from Friday. You'll eat well for a change."

"So who was it? Chip Carswell doing penance?"

Allison casually took a sip of lemonade. "No, it wasn't your pal Chip the roving reporter. As a matter of fact, it was Jacqueline Stilwell."

"What? Are you serious?"

"Apparently she wants to talk about Irish Wolf hounds some more. She apologized for sending me away so abruptly. Oh, and she said it was all right if I brought you along provided you didn't bring a shovel."

"But I thought she hated me," said Max, still amazed.

"Well, the jury is still out on that question. I'd advise being on your best behavior. There's plenty of room for new holes at Casa Leone."

Max put his arm around her. "You know, Allison, I always thought we made a good team. And once again, you've proven it."

She smiled. "Flattery will get you everywhere."

*John Reisinger*

## Chapter 5
## The scene of the crime

# 1926

The Stilwell Building stood on the corner across from the old courthouse in the business center of Easton. It was three stories high and broken up into offices and small business tenants. Formerly a hotel, it had been taken over and renovated by the Stilwells. The Stilwell Building was now the prestige address in town and commanded the highest rents.

Max parked in front of the courthouse and he and Allison made their way through a crowd of curious onlookers to the door of the Stilwell Building. They climbed the stairs and came upon another group of people. All the heads turned and looked at them simultaneously. The crowd parted as they approached. A policeman standing guard in front of the door of Chesapeake Investments let them in the office and the crowd closed up behind them again.

"Max, Allison. I'm glad you're here," said Chief Vickers, kneeling by a body. "Take a look."

Max squatted down and saw the body of a middle aged man with thinning brown hair. He was lying on his back and was very dead. There were three small, ugly bullet holes, two in the chest and one in the forearm. The hole in the forearm showed dark smudges of a powder burn, but the others didn't.

"The bullet in the arm passed through. If we can find where it hit in the office, we can trace the trajectory and maybe tell where the killer was standing," said Vickers.

"Maybe," said Max, "but I wouldn't bet on finding any bullet in the wall. The entry wound is on the palm side of the forearm, so he was holding his arm up in a defensive position when he was shot. That bullet is one of the ones in his chest."

"So there were only two shots?"

"Apparently. Anything in his pockets?"

"Some odds and ends. We're going through them now. He had a locked strongbox he kept in the closet and it wasn't touched. He had about $500 in it, so it looks like it wasn't a robbery, that is, assuming the killer knew it was there."

"Let me look around and get my bearings," said Max, walking around the office. The main room, where the body was, had a desk on one side, along with several tables and chairs. On the desk were several stacks of three by five inch papers that looked like forms or certificates of some kind. Max glanced at them and found each one contained the name of a stock, a number of shares of the stock, a date, and someone's name, presumably a client.

"So Charles Leroux was a stockbroker?" Max asked.

Vickers looked up. "More or less. Chesapeake Investments was a bucket shop."

"A what?"

"It was sort of news to me, too, Max. Officer DeGrange filled me in. It seems that the stock market is going great guns and lots of people want in on it. Problem is, a stockbroker will charge you a hefty commission and require you to buy a round lot...that's  multiples of 100 shares. Not many people have that kind of money to invest, so a bucket shop allows them to buy just a few shares with a small commission. That way just about anyone can play the stock market."

"But how can a bucket shop man buy small amounts of stocks for such a low commission?" Max asked.

"Because he doesn't actually buy anything. A bucket shop acts as sort of a betting parlor. You get a slip that documents the stock you chose and what you paid based on the price of that stock at the time. If the price goes up and you resell it, you make a profit, if it goes down, you lose. So Leroux was acting as a bookie for stocks. His commission, coupled with the proceeds of the stocks that went down  was enough to cover the ones that went up. Capitalism at its finest."

"That explains all the stock slips," said Max.

Allison, meanwhile, was looking at the small room in the back, the only one with a window, though the window was barred. Along one wall was a table and several rows of shelves with books of stock information. In the corner was a closet with a broom, dustpan, some empty boxes, and a tin trash can. Allison was careful not to touch anything, and went back in the outer office.

She found Max looking at a large chalkboard on one wall. The board was divided into neat rows and columns with three headings; Security, Latest Price, and Notes.

Allison stopped beside Max and read the names on the rows.

"Allied Chemical, American Can, American Car and Foundry, Mack Trucks, Sears Roebuck, US Steel, Woolworth....These look like stocks. The Dow Industrials, to be precise. It looks like he updated the prices pretty frequently for his clients."

Max looked at her. "How do you know about the Dow Industrial Index?"

"Any reason I shouldn't?"

Max chuckled. "None whatsoever. I don't know why anything you say should surprise me."

Max went back to the desk and opened the drawers. In the upper right drawer was a personal journal lying on top of another small pile of the ubiquitous three by five stock slips. A quick glance revealed that these slips all had VOID stamped on them. Max thumbed through the book.

"There is no entry for yesterday, just the day before that. It looks like pretty routine stuff; records of visitors and who bought or sold how many shares. Maybe there's an entry that says so-and-so stopped by and said he was coming back later to shoot me. Hmmm...no such luck. There are no entries for today at all."

Chief Vickers was now standing. "I went through that journal just before you arrived, Max. It's dull as dirt. There was one entry about an unhappy client demanding his money back last week, but otherwise, nothing remotely related to murder."

Max nodded. "So it seems." He put the book aside and looked at the slips in the bottom of the drawer.

"These seem to be completed transactions, and they're all for small sums. Nothing to get shot over." He placed the slips and journal back and opened the next drawer.

"Hello, what's this? Our victim had a cultural side? It looks like a book of old paintings. Color pictures, too. No notes or inscriptions. Unusual, but nothing startling."

The rest of the drawers yielded stacks of blank stock slips, some pens, pencils and chalk for the tally board, and finally, some personal receipts and bills.

"Not much we can get out teeth into," said Vickers, gloomily. "There's a trash can in the closet, along with a box of tools. The trash can has some broken brick pieces and sand in it."

Max turned his head. "Brick pieces and sand? Now where would that come from? Let me see this trash can."

Max went in the back room and examined the trash can Allison has seen earlier. As Vickers had said, it was about a third full of broken bits of brick, sand, and mortar. On the other side of the closet was a small box containing a hammer, a trowel, and a chisel.

"Now, this is interesting," said Max. "Why the tools and the pieces of brick in the waste can? Leroux wasn't in the construction business."

Max looked around both rooms and found an empty wooden crate against the wall by the window. He pulled it aside and saw an area of the wall that had been cracked and chiseled.

"This explains the tools and the debris in the trash can," said Allison. "It looks like he was trying to make room for a bigger window, but he was renting the space.

57

What did he expect Glenn Stilwell would do when he found out?"

Chief Vickers appeared. "Well, I doubt he was killed over unauthorized renovations."

"Probably not," Max agreed, "but it's odd none the less. Have you talked to the other tenants?"

"We're making arrangements now," said Vickers. "There's a conference room two doors down. We can do interviews there. I'd appreciate it if you could sit in, Max."

Marsha Tolley of Tolley Real Estate sat rigidly at the table with her hands folded, as if she were in the schoolroom of a particularly demanding teacher. Her bobbed red hair caught the light from a nearby window as she reminisced about her late neighbor.

"Mr. Leroux was a nice man. He was French Canadian, or maybe just French. I never could tell the difference, to tell you the truth. He never said, but he had an accent. He used to say hello every morning and sometimes stopped by for coffee."

"Did he have many visitors?" Vickers asked.

"Oh, yes. He had people traipsing in and out all the time. That's probably why he worked at night so much; just to catch up."

"Did any of his clients express dissatisfaction that you know of?" Max asked.

"Just one, Harold Santino. Charles used to talk about him a lot. He used to buy on margin; you know, with borrowed money. Well, that is fine so long as the stock goes up, but when it goes down, you lose money even faster. Well that Harold Santino used to borrow to buy every stock he could get his hands on. He kept picking losers and didn't take it well; accused poor Mr. Leroux of rigging the numbers. He demanded his money back and said he'd get it back one way or another."

"Was Mr. Leroux concerned?" Max asked.

"Obviously, he had good reason to be," said Mrs. Tolley, shaking her head.


Grayson Dunlop, the tax accountant nervously lit a cigarette. "Look, I don't know what happened. On day he was here, and the next he was dead. I don't know who did it. I don't even know *how* they did it."

"Did you invest with Mr. Leroux?" Vickers asked.

"Sure; I took a flyer now and then."

"How did you do?"

Dunlop shrugged. "I lost some, but that's the breaks."

"So how much did you lose?" said Max.

"Oh, I don't remember exactly, but it wasn't much, maybe a few sawbucks worth."

"Do you know who might have wanted to kill Leroux?"

"No, but I didn't know many of his clients. Anything's possible, I guess. I mean, when you deal in other people's money, sometimes you have to give them bad news. I should know; I'm an accountant. And when you give people bad news about their money, well..."

Well what?"

"You make enemies."

## Chapter 6
## Glenn Stilwell drops in

Max, Allison and Chief Vickers were standing in the hallway after the interviews comparing notes when the sound of heavy footsteps told them someone was coming and coming in a hurry.

A large man with jet black hair and a patch over one eye appeared. "Vickers! Just what is going on here? Has someone been murdered in my building?"

"Morning Mr. Stilwell," said Vickers. "Yes, I'm afraid it's true. Mr. Charles Leroux of Chesapeake Investments. We're investigating right now. Mr. Hurlock is assisting."

Stilwell glanced at Max as if noticing him and Allison for the first time. "Oh. Good morning Max. Good morning Allison. Do you know who did it yet?"

"Not yet, Mr. Stilwell. Mr. Leroux had contacts with a lot of people."

"Well, I don't need this publicity. This is a prestige address, not a gangster haven. I have to rent these spaces, and that'll be a lot harder if prospective tenants think they'd be taking their life in their hands. I want whoever did this found and hanged!"

"We may have to have a trial first," said Allison, under her breath.

Max put on his smoothest, most soothing manner. "Mr. Stilwell, we will do our best, but maybe you can help us. You know more about this building and its tenants than anyone. "

"Yes, I suppose I do," Stilwell conceded. "What do you want to know?"

"What can you tell us about Mr. Leroux's background?"

Glenn Stilwell sat in an office chair and wrinkled his brow. "As far as I know he was French; came over after the war sometime and settled in Philadelphia with his wife. He never seemed to be short of cash and I got the impression he had some sort of private means, maybe an inheritance or something like that. He had some sort of falling out with his wife and she stayed in Philadelphia. He told me he wanted to make a fresh start and thought the Eastern Shore had a lot of potential. Chesapeake Investments wasn't a proper stockbroker; it was what they call a bucket shop. It acted as more of a betting parlor based on stock movements. He said he wanted to start small and work his way to something bigger."

"How long was Mr. Leroux's lease?"

"Month to month."

"Wasn't that unusual for a business that deals with handling money from the public?" said Max.

Stilwell nodded. "I asked the same thing, but he said he was looking for a bigger place with ground floor access and this was just to get established."

"So you met with him before he signed his lease?"

"I meet with every tenant," said Stilwell. "That's how I keep out the riff raff. That's the main reason I have an office in the building, although I don't go there much. I sit down with each tenant and size them up. Then, if I approve, we look over a floor plan for the building to make sure he's satisfied with his space. That avoids disappointment later. Then we inspect the space he selects and sign the papers."

"Did he ever talk about his wife?"

"Not much. It seemed like a sore subject to him. I heard rumors that he was carrying on with several local woman, but I don't really know for sure."

"Were you aware he was putting in a new window in the back?"

Stilwell shook his head. "New window? No, that was not a new window. The sill and some of the brickwork had been damaged by the previous tenant and needed to be replaced. Leroux offered to do it for a free month and I agreed."

"Did you know anyone who might have wanted him dead?"

"Maybe his wife, or some of his less fortunate clients, I suppose. Some of them claimed he doctored the stock prices he got off the ticker, but I never saw any evidence of it. Just sour grapes, if you ask me. Look, you have to find this killer and find him fast."

"We're on it," said Max. "Allison is helping out as well."

"Good. Keep me informed. I'll be watching and I am not known for my patience."

He tipped his hat to Allison, spun on his heel, and was gone.

"Well, Max," said Chief Vickers, "We're in for it now. We have a man killed in Stilwell's building and we don't know why he was killed, who killed him, or even how it was done. The only clues we have are confusing and contradictory. And we have Glenn Stilwell breathing down our necks."

Max smiled. "Yes, but there are answers out there. All we have to do is find them."

"Oh, is that all? What a relief. I was getting worried. So what do we do now?"

"I would suggest you seal off this space and have someone go through the ledger entries in detail to see if anything interesting  pops up, such as someone who lost a lot of money or some record of a disgruntled visitor. Meanwhile, I'm going to see a man about a painting."


Max and Allison made their way out of the building, walked up the street past the curious crowd and compared notes.

"There's an art gallery about a block over that might have some information about this book that was in Leroux's office," Max said. "I don't know if the book has anything to do with the case, but I'd like to get any background I can. Want to come along?"

"I don't think so; two people showing up with questions might cause them to panic or clam up," Allison said. "I think I'll stay here a bit. I saw an interesting name on the list of tenants I'd like to know more about. There might be an article in it."

"All right. I'll meet you at the car in an hour."

Allison threaded her way through the crowd to the first floor of the Stilwell Building and found the office door with the sign reading "Chesapeake Bridge Company".

"Surely they can't mean a bridge across the entire bay?" she said aloud, then opened the door and walked in. A small bald man in a vest sat at a cluttered desk in a small room surrounded by maps, railroad timetables, and sketches of trains and bridges. He jerked his head up, looked startled, then smiled, as if he had always prayed a beautiful woman would one day walk through that door, and now it had finally happened.

"Oh...hello. Can I help you....Miss?" the man at the Chesapeake Bridge Company asked.

"Hello. I'm Allison Hurlock," she replied, "and I was wondering about your company. Do you really intend to build a bridge across the bay?"

"Are you a reporter?" he asked hopefully.

"Not at the moment, but I write for several magazines. So are you going to build a bridge or not?"

The man brightened up even more.

"Absolutely! We'll connect the two halves of Maryland for the first time. It will enrich everyone. Twenty seven feet wide and eight miles long is the plan, enough for two lanes. The Eastern Shore is cut off from the rest of the state by the Chesapeake Bay, but the Eastern Shore produces great quantities of agricultural products, seafood, and poultry. So what do they do with it?"

"Well, they..."

"Exactly! They send it north to Wilmington and Philadelphia because that's where the railroads go. And the railroads go that way because there is now no way to get bulk products across the bay efficiently. Baltimore, Annapolis and Washington only get the part that comes by boat. When the bridge is built, however, Baltimore, Annapolis and Washington will become part of the market for the Eastern Shore. Say, do you think you'll write an article about us?"

Allison smiled. "You never know, but I would have to find more information first."

The man nodded rapidly, as if his head was loose.

"Certainly. Of course." He started rummaging through some papers on his desk. "Here is a brochure we give to potential investors. My name is Will Purdum. I'm the Eastern Shore Coordinator. I'm lining up investors, farmers, and canneries to sign on with this little venture so it'll be all set to begin operations once the bridge is built. An article from you would help get the word out."

Allison thumbed through the brochure.

"It looks like it will be up at Tolchester and Rock Hall. I suppose that's the narrowest part of the bay."

"Not exactly the narrowest, but it will connect the Eastern Shore with Baltimore."

"Sounds expensive, though."

"We have a team drawing up plans now, so we will see, but the untapped market is huge. You will let me know if you write an article?"

"Of course. Thank you, Mr. Purdum. I may call on you again."

Mr. Purdum's face lit up. "That would be wonderful, Miss Hurlock."

"It's Mrs."

"Oh. Well, stop by anytime."


The Kirby Gallery on Washington Street was the only place in Easton someone could talk about painting that didn't involve a barn. On the walls were various depictions of boats, ducks, marshland, and sunsets over water. The owner, Cal Kirby, looked up hopefully when Max appeared in his doorway.

"Good morning, sir. In the market for a fine painting?"

"Just for some art enlightenment today, I'm afraid," said Max.

Kirby's face fell. "Enlightenment?"

"I'm Max Hurlock. I'm helping the police in an investigation and I'm interested in this art book they turned up. What can you tell me about it?"

Max placed the book on the table. Kirby looked at it and flipped a few pages.

"This is fine stuff, Mr. Hurlock...Museum quality... old masters and the like. It's a bit high end for my gallery, I'm afraid. I don't deal in paintings like this. I can't afford it. My clientele is mostly wealthy business people who have summer homes around here and want some art for the walls. Their tastes run to ducks, egrets, boats and riverscapes. Still, there is some fine work being done by local artists in this area."

"But nothing like the paintings in this book?"

"Oh, occasionally someone will want a formal oil portrait of himself or his family done in the classic style, but this book has mostly religious inspired art from Europe. No one has any of that around here as far as I know. If they do, they didn't purchase it from me. Only a church would be interested and a church couldn't afford this level."

"So, if someone had a book like this in his office, what would it mean?"

Kirby shrugged. "Only that he has some interest in art, or maybe in old books."

"It couldn't mean he was looking to purchase one of these works?"

"I doubt that any of these are for sale. Besides, anyone contemplating a high end art purchase wouldn't be using a picture book, he'd have a catalogue with a detailed description from whatever gallery had it."

"Is there anything really unusual or interesting about any of the paintings?"

"Each one is interesting in its own way, of course, but, as I said, it's not really my area of expertise, and I'm afraid this is the only gallery in town."

"Oh, well," said Max. "It was worth a try. Thanks for your time."

Kirby snapped his fingers. "Wait a second. You know, you might be in luck after all. Nigel Smythe-Cunningham is in town...or at least he was a few days ago. He runs one of the biggest galleries in New York...knows absolutely everything about the old masters and classic art. He can afford it up in New York. Anyway, he stopped by the other day to look at my wildlife paintings. I don't know if he's still around or not, but he was staying at the Avon."

"He sounds like my man," said Max, "but what's he doing on the Eastern Shore?"

"You may have read that Mr. Perryman of Perryman's Products just died. He had retired to a place near Oxford. The executors called in Mr. Smythe-Cunningham to appraise the art that was part of the estate. Smythe-Cunningham is the man to go to for estate appraisals all over the country. "

When Max made the short walk to the Avon Hotel, the desk clerk confirmed that Mr. Smythe-Cunningham was still checked in, but was out and not expected back until after noon. Max met Allison back at the car.

"An out of town art expert, eh," said Allison. "Of course, I suppose you realize that the painting book probably has absolutely nothing to do with this case."

Max nodded. "Almost certainly, but I thought I could at least eliminate it from the evidence mix. How about you? What was that place you were interested in?"

"It's a group trying to build a bridge over the bay."

"I heard something about that," said Max. "It sounded a little pie in the sky to me. Still, it's an interesting idea. You think there's an article in it for you?"

"Maybe. I thought I'd get some different views on the effect of a bridge across the bay. You know; farmers, watermen, marina owners, and some of the landlords in Ocean City."

Max nodded. "It's a good angle. Even if the bridge doesn't get built, I'd bet that one day there will be a bridge of some kind. From an engineering point of view, it's almost inevitable."

"I figured you could help me with any technical questions."

"Sure; sounds like an interesting article."

"Well, they can't all be about flappers. So are you going to track down this Smythe-Whatshisname bird?"

"I don't know. I really should, I guess, but I'm afraid it will be a waste of time. Anyway, it's a low priority right now. Let me check back with the chief before we go."

"I'll meet you back at the car in about an hour, said Allison. I think I'll mingle with the crowd and see if I overhear something interesting."

"All right, but take it easy," said Max, smiling. "Remember, you're snooping for two now."

"I was snooping for two all along," Allison retorted, and turned back towards the Stilwell building.

On the second floor, she found people still milling around in the corridor and stealing glances into the partially open door of Chesapeake Investments. Several men had arrived to take the body away, starting the chatter and speculation all over again.

"I hear he was shot twelve times."

"I heard he was stabbed, too."

"Naw, I heard it was suicide. It had to be; the room was locked."

Amidst the cloud of uninformed speculation, Allison spotted a woman about her age who was very pregnant, maybe eight months' worth. The woman smiled and shook her head when Allison caught her eye.

"This is just what junior needs," she said, patting her stomach, "fear and confusion."

Allison smiled. "I'm expecting as well, but not for another eight months or so. Is this your first?"

"My fourth. I don't envy you, honey. My first one was the worst. I was in hard labor for a whole night. And the pain! I was cursing my husband, my god, and every male who was ever born or ever *would* be born."

Allison was momentarily shocked into silence.

"Now you take my cousin, Hattie over to Cambridge. Her baby's had every childhood disease known to man and a few that aren't...and Hattie has to clean up the mess nearly every day. And my aunt had a daughter that was never right in the head from the day she was born. I'm telling you, honey, this is just the calm before the storm."

"Well, I don't think...."

"And the screaming and crying all the time! I'm telling you the only reason the Good Lord made babies look cute is so their parents wouldn't strangle 'em. Even so, it's pretty close sometimes."

Allison was discretely backing away and was about to excuse herself, when the woman abruptly changed the subject.

"Isn't it awful about Mr. Leroux? Not that I was all that surprised."

Allison stopped. "Not surprised? Why is that?"

71

The woman affected an all-knowing expression and lowered her voice. "Well, come on; Mr. Leroux was not everyone's favorite around here. Grayson Dunlop used to grumble about him all the time, ever since he lost all that money with him. Then there was Marsha Tolley."

"The real estate lady?" said Allison. "Did she lose money as well?"

"Oh, she lost more than that, dear. She was very friendly with Mr. Leroux, if you know what I mean. She figured he'd marry her once his divorce became final, but that still hasn't happened, and Mr. Leroux was in no hurry. Marsha was starting to realize she was being played for a sucker and she wasn't too happy about it. I hear she even saw him with yet another woman; someone named Violet."

"Do you know Violet's last name?"

"No, I never heard a last name."

"And you think Marsha Tolley was mad enough to kill him?" Allison tried not to look too amazed.

"I couldn't say. All I know is that I worked late yesterday and left around seven thirty. Mr. Leroux's light was on and so was Marsha Tolley's. You can tell by the transoms, you know. So for a while, at least, she was the only one in the building with him. A few hours later, he's dead. Quite a coincidence if you want my opinion."

The chief was back at the police station past the old courthouse a few blocks away. Max found Vickers in a back room with piles of papers.

"Max! Am I glad to see you."

"What's going on, Chief?" Max asked.

"I've had my best men going through the papers we found in Leroux's desk and found some very interesting things."

"I'm all ears."

"You recall Leroux had a book that was a combination ledger and diary. He kept track of who held what stock slips and also kept notes in the same book. Well, it seems that both Harold Santino and Grayson Dunlop lost money with Leroux."

"We knew that," said Max. "Santino lost a lot and was angry about it. Dunlop lost some, but didn't seem worried about it."

"That's what we thought, all right, but we had it backwards. Santino lost $375 over the course of about six months, but Dunlop lost almost $3,000. But Santino is upset and Dunlop just shrugs it off. Can you beat that?"

"Interesting," said Max, "but it might have something to do with Santino's suspicions of double dealing by Leroux. Getting cheated out of a small amount might seem worse than losing more but losing it fair and square."

"Yeah, maybe. We also found some papers and letters from his wife down on D.C. She's a stenographer for some agency or other. It seems the Lerouxs were in the midst of a rather messy divorce."

"What was the issue?" said Max.

"The letters don't really go into detail. She just makes references to his 'outside interests'. I'm betting those 'outside interests' wear skirts."

"Wouldn't be the first time," said Max. "Maybe we should talk to Mrs. Leroux."

"I have someone trying to track her down now," said Vickers.

An officer stuck his head in the door. "Chief, there's a telephone call for you. It's Mr. Stilwell."

Vickers looked at Max and sighed. "And so it begins; the first of many calls. He'll be demanding hour by hour updates."

"Well, we'll just have to get this thing solved then," said Max.

## Chapter 7

## An out of town expert

When Max got back to the car, he found Allison waiting for him.

"Hey, Max. I've got a lot to tell you, but it's past lunch time. How about grabbing a bite at the Avon Hotel?"

"Sure. I think they have soft crabs today."

Allison nodded. "That's a good combination; soft crabs to take the edge off hard cases."

In the dining room of the Avon Hotel, the murmured conversations, blended with the clink of plates and glasses, softly rose and fell among the potted palms and dark wood paneling of the dining room to create a soothing effect. The conversation, between Max and Allison, however, was serious.

"I met this woman at the Stilwell building who felt compelled to tell me horror stories of childbirth disasters," Allison began, looking at the menu. "I have no idea why people do that, but I wish they would stop. I mean, if they are trying to warn me, it's too late."

Max smiled. "There are always people who try to top you, no matter what the occasion. I knew a guy in high school like that. We called him 'That's Nothin' because he would start almost every sentence with that phrase. If you

75

said you got bitten by a dog, he'd say 'That's nothin'; I was once eaten by a bear!'. Nobody took him seriously."

"It's still pretty annoying," said Allison. "Anyway, she also said that Marsha Tolley, the real estate lady in the Stilwell Building was carrying on with Leroux and was pretty unhappy with his foot dragging on his divorce. She says Tolley saw him with yet another woman, someone called Violet. She also claims Tolley and Leroux were the only two in the building around seven or so when she left.

"So Marsha Tolley was seeing Leroux and felt jilted, eh?" Max said. "A lot of people have killed for less. And I wonder who this Violet woman might be?"

"Assuming she actually exists," said Allison.

"Well," said Max, putting the menu down, "I found out that Grayson Dunlop lost $3,000 with Leroux."

"Really? He didn't act like it. So we have three people with possible motives right off the bat, Grayson Dunlop, Marsha Tolley, and Harold Santino."

"Maybe even one more," said Max. "Leroux's wife seemed none too pleased with him either. They were going through a divorce. It sounds like Charles Leroux had a roving eye."

Max ordered, then shook his head slowly. "So now we have Marsha Tolley, Grayson Dunlop, Harold Santino, Mrs. Leroux, and possibly this mysterious Violet person with possible motives."

"Well, you're the detective, darling," said Allison, "but I thought the object was to *narrow* the list of suspects."

They changed the subject and the rest of the meal went much smoother, especially after the soft crabs arrived. Soon, the unpleasant business at the Stilwell Building was pushed into the background, and they were feeling content and carefree as they crossed the lobby towards the front door.

"Mr. Hurlock?" came a voice behind them. Max and Allison turned to see a short rotund man wearing a dark suit with a red carnation. He carried a cane and wore a pair of pince-nez glasses attached to a black ribbon.

"The lad at the front desk pointed you out and said you wished to speak to me. Mr. Nigel Smythe-Cunningham of the Smythe-Cunningham Galley in New York at your service." The man spoke with an upper class British accent that would not have been out of place at Eton.

"Oh, yes," said Max. "This is my wife Allison."

Mr. Smythe-Cunningham bowed at the waist. "Charming; simply charming. Am I correct in assuming you are interested in fine art?"

"Maybe we can have a seat over by that fireplace," said Max. They sat in a grouping of overstuffed chairs near the door.

"Mr. Smythe-..."

"Cunningham."

"Yes. Well, the fact is, we are not interested in art as a purchase."

Mr. Smythe-Cunningham's face fell slightly. "I see. Pity."

"But," Max continued, "we would appreciate your opinion on an art-related matter. You see there has been a murder..."

Smythe-Cunningham's eyebrows raised in surprise. "A murder? In Easton? Oh, surely not."

"Does that surprise you?" Allison asked.

"Astonish is more the *mot jus*. Being from New York, I have come to regard Easton as downright bucolic, wot?"

"Not this time, I'm afraid," said Max. "A stockbroker has been killed at the Stilwell Building near the courthouse... in a locked room."

"A murder in a locked room? Oh, I say. How exciting! I mean, bad luck for the deceased and all that, but I do have a soft spot for mysteries; I read them constantly. A bit of the old deduction, wot? It sounds like *The Big Bow Mystery* by Israel Zangwill. But surely you're not with the police?"

"No" said Max. "I'm a civilian, but I am helping the police investigate."

"Capitol!" Mr. Smythe-Cunningham actually slapped his knee. "The gifted amateur assisting the authorities in their inquiries. Agatha Christie writ large. Oh, this is delicious. How can I help? I do so enjoy a good murder."

Allison looked shocked, and Smythe-Cunningham backtracked. "Oh, I don't mean to cheer sudden death, my dear. I am simply a fan of the mystery genre. I must have read them all. I enjoy the logical puzzle; the game of wits involved, but I've never been involved in one in real life, so you must forgive me my enthusiasm."

He turned to Max. "Then you must be the fabled amateur sleuth in this case. Oh, this is topping; first-rate. Can you demonstrate your deductive ability?"

"Mr. Smythe-Cunningham...."

"Oh, do call me Nigel, but what about that deduction?"

Max sighed. "Oh, all right." He looked Smythe-Cunningham over closely. "Why did you shave off your mustache?"

Mr. Smythe-Cunningham sat frozen for a moment, then grinned. "Good show! I usually have a mustache but I have been thinking of shaving it off to look a bit more modern. When I arrived in Maryland and experienced the heat and humidity in your fair state a few days ago, I finally took the plunge and got rid of it. But how did you know?"

"The area above your lip is several shades paler than the rest of your face."

"Bravo! I'm in the presence of a real detective. This is marvelous. How may I help? Is the crime related to art in some way?"

"Probably not," said Max, "but we did find this book in the victim's desk and I wondered if it might mean anything. It seemed a bit out of place for a stockbroker's office."

Max produced the art book and handed it to Nigel, who thumbed through the pages thoughtfully. "Oh, yes; *Masterpieces of the Renaissance*. I am quite familiar with this book. It's a collection of mostly religious painting from that period. Rather good reproductions. Mind you, the pictures don't compare with the originals. Did he have any other art books in his possession?"

"We didn't find any. Any idea why a stockbroker would have a book like this?" said Max.

Mr. Smythe-Cunningham looked disappointed. "In fact, I do. You recall, I'm sure, the theft of the Mona Lisa from the Louvre in 1911?"

"Of course," Max and Allison said simultaneously.

"A rum business. Turned out it was an Italian cleaning man who hid it in his apartment. They finally recovered it two years later when the rascal tried to sell it to the Uffizi in Florence. Anyway, you may recall, the publicity from that crime was tremendous. People all over the world knew about it. Well, one of the more fortunate side effects, at least from my point of view, was a resurgence of public interest in art, particularly the European masters." He gestured with the book.

"This book was published in 1912 to help meet the demand, and provide novices with a quick reference. It sold quite well, in fact. I have a copy, myself, and I have seen it in shops, hotels, restaurants, and private homes all over. So, much as I'd like to help you find a vital clue, I must tell you that the presence of this book is indicative of nothing beyond a casual interest in art. Its presence in a stockbroker's office strikes me as nothing unusual. Had the victim a serious interest in art, I would expect him to possess some of the more comprehensive and detailed works that are available, but you said there was nothing of that sort at the scene. No, I'm afraid this particular book is nothing more than what the mystery writers would call a red herring, a false lead. Sorry."

Max sat back in his chair. "That's pretty much what I figured, but it's good to hear it from an expert."

Smythe-Cunningham looked apologetic. "Oh, I say; dash it all, I wish I could turn up a vital clue for you, but I see nothing unusual about that book. It even appears to be devoid of notes or underlining, or anything to indicate the victim even read it. Dashed disappointing and all that, but I will be in town until Friday, so if you find anything else, I would be glad to help."

"Thank you. If anything art-related turns up, you will be the first to know."

Out on the sidewalk, Max and Allison turned to each other.

"We keep getting more suspects, but fewer clues," said Max. "We're losing ground."


On the way back to St Michaels, Max and Allison stopped at Bemis's General Store for some groceries. Betty Bemis spotted them and descended on Allison.

"Oh, Allison. Have you had morning sickness yet?"

"It's only the second month, Betty."

"Lands! When I was pregnant with Billy, I was throwing up so much I thought I'd turn inside out. I threw up things I'd eaten back in high school. It was like some great hand was wringing me out. And cramps? I was rolling on the floor in agony when I wasn't bent over the toilet."

"Betty..."

"Now, what groceries can I get you?"

"Maybe just a box of crackers."

Back home, Allison slumped into a wicker chair on the front porch and looked weary.

"Max, why do women try to undermine one of their own? Why can't they encourage me instead of hanging out a sign that says 'Abandon hope, all ye who enter here.' Misery doesn't just love company, it insists on it."

"You're asking me to explain women to you?" Max asked.

Allison smiled. "No; I'm just grousing out loud. Let's talk about something else."

"All right," said Max. "I'm not an authority on female psychology anyway. So what did you think of Mr...what was it?...Smythe-Cunningam?"

"A nice enough man, and very knowledgeable, but a bit superficial."

"You mean phony?"

"No, not phony really, just, well, exaggerated a bit...almost flamboyant. I mean, the man has run a big gallery in New York for years, but he still sounds as if he's addressing the House of Parliament."

Max laughed. "Nothing unusual there. He's a salesman. The man sells fancy art works to the upper crust. I imagine the British accent and mannerisms are part of the show, and enhance the air of snobbish sophistication his patrons appreciate. It's not phony, exactly, just playing to his audience. If he worked in a factory, he would have lost much of the accent by now."

Allison rose from the chair and went to the icebox to get some lemonade. Although Allison's cooking was erratic at best, her lemonade was always first rate. The afternoon sun was as warm as ever and the cicadas in the trees outside were chirping furiously. Max and Allison sat on the familiar wicker chairs on the porch and sipped moodily.

"Do you think the baby will change our life?" she said, finally.

"Well, of course. Isn't that the whole point?"

"No, I mean you and me. Will we still have each other?"

"What are you talking about?"

Allison took another sip and looked off into the middle distance. "Look, I don't take all the horror stories seriously, but they got me to thinking about us. We've been free to go and do what we wanted up until now and it's been great, but that's going to change. After the baby comes, will that spark still be there?"

Max reached over and grasped her hand. "Was it there when you pulled into that repair garage on a rainy night? Was it there when I was in the Navy and you were working at the Sunpapers? Was it there when I was stuck in France and didn't know when I'd ever get back? We've been through a war together. It'll take more than some runny-nosed half-pint in diapers to pry us apart."

She squeezed his hand and smiled. "Don't mind me. I guess my chemistry is out of whack at the moment. I'll get back on my bridge article and I'll be fine."

"So are you pursuing the bridge article, then?"

"I think so. The trick will be getting enough information and making it interesting to the average reader, but I think it's a timely topic."

Max nodded. "I've been tied up on that road realignment over towards Denton, but I'll nose around and see if there is any engineering proposal yet. I know most of the engineering design firms on the shore."

"I think for something this big, the Baltimore firms will be used," Allison said. "I'm sure the Port of Baltimore interests are behind it. I may have to go there before it's over. I don't suppose you'll need me here now that the art angle has been shot down."

Max grinned. "I always need you here, but I'll spare you for a day or so in the interests of the article."

"In that case...is that the phone?"

"Want me to get it?" said Max.

"No," said Allison, rising from the chair. "I have to put the lemonade away anyway."

She returned a minute later. "That was Jacqueline Stilwell. She invited us to dinner tonight at Casa Leone."

"Tonight? It's almost four o'clock already. Isn't that pretty short notice?"

"She apologized for the notice, but said she had something to discuss."

"I'll bet she has; something about people getting murdered at their office building, no doubt. So do you want to go?"

Allison shrugged. "I don't see how we can resist."

## Chapter 8

## Dinner at Casa Leone

Casa Leone was at the end of a long road near Bellevue, opposite the sleepy town of Oxford and about 20 minutes from St Michaels. Two guards greeted Max and Allison at a brick gatehouse and opened a heavy cast iron gate across the driveway. The Model A proceeded down a lane overhung by shade trees.

"I suppose they don't encourage drop ins," Max observed, as the gates closed behind them.

The lane took a slow turn and Casa Leone came into view, a stately, three story tan stucco building with a central bell tower and red tile roof. The gracious architecture, with its various levels, arches, shutters, patios, balconies, statues, and manicured plantings was classic Italianate, like some Doge's Palace in Venice. The house stood facing formal gardens laid out around a pond with a fountain quietly splashing away in its center. Beyond the gardens, the Tred Avon River sparkled silently in the middle distance, aloof to the luxury along its shore. A wide wooden pier jutted out with a large black sailboat tied at the end.

"Be it ever so humble," Allison said quietly, as if afraid of being overheard.

"Don't tell Nigel Smythe-Cunningham about this place," said Max. "He'd be pounding on the gates to try to sell them paintings."

They parked the car and climbed a wide stone stairway to an even wider stone porch that was more like a plaza, lined with classical statues. The carved wooden front doors of Casa Leone were ten feet high and framed by a carved stone archway. Max pulled a bell cord and they heard a bell ring somewhere deep inside the house.

"Shouldn't we be using the servants' entrance?" Max asked.

"Shush," said Allison.

The heavy wooden doors opened, and Jacqueline Stilwell greeted them. She was tall and aristocratic, with the sort of bearing that hinted she was about to order a peasant to be flogged.

"Ah, the Hurlocks. How nice to see you again. Please come in."

"Good to see you, Mrs. Stilwell," said Max, smiling.

"I'm so glad you were free on such short notice," said Mrs. Stilwell.

"Yes," said Max. "Fortunately our engagement with the Duke of Edinburgh was cancelled at the last minute....Ow!"

Max rubbed his leg where Allison had just kicked him.


The entrance hall led into a baronial living room with a massive stone fireplace, tapestries, and two stained glass windows. Henry the Eighth would have felt right at home.

"My husband will not be joining us tonight," Mrs. Stilwell continued. "He's dining with the Chairman of the Board of the Star-Democrat so they can discuss the coverage of the unfortunate incident today."

Max looked at Allison, but did not reply. No one had to ask exactly what unfortunate incident she had in mind.

"Allison and Max, I'm sure you remember our estate manager, Mr. Ned Gunther?"

She indicated the burly bald man standing stiffly by the fireplace.

"Of course," said Max, extending his hand. How are you, Mr. Gunther?"

A servant girl materialized with a tray of drinks and the party was seated.

"The place looks lovely, Mrs. Stilwell," said Allison. "We haven't been here since...well, you know."

"We can speak of that later," said Mrs. Stilwell. "Casa Leone has only improved since that time. That tapestry over the fireplace, for instance is new, and, of course, the gardens have flourished."

"And how are the Irish Wolfhounds?"

"Splendid," said Mrs. Stilwell, who then launched into a long history of her adventures in dog breeding. Presently, dinner was announced and they took their places at the table in the adjoining room. The dining room at Casa Leone was two stories high and seemed to revolve around a massive chandelier hanging in the center. Along the walls were several paintings, tapestries and sconces, as well as another stone fireplace, complete with crackling fire. The room seemed to have been lifted intact from some Renaissance palace. High-backed carved wooden chairs stood at a heavy oak dining table set for four, with a bewildering assortment of plates, glasses, and silverware.

After the appetizers, Mrs. Stilwell daubed her mouth and cleared her throat delicately.

"I suppose you're wondering about the *raison d'etre* of this occasion."

"Well, not really," said Max. "You're concerned about the unpleasantness at the Stilwell building this morning."

"Er...yes. Of course," said Mrs. Stilwell, recovering quickly. "No one knows just what happened yet, but the potential for ugly publicity is great. My purpose in asking you both here this evening, aside from the pleasant company you provide, is to plead with you to dispose of this case as expeditiously as possible and to do it discretely."

"That's the way I handle every case, Mrs. Stilwell," Max reminded her.

"Ditto," said Allison.

"I'm counting on it, Max. I will never forget that awful incident several years ago, when the Police chief...what was his name?"

"Tom Vickers."

"Yes, of course, Chief Vickers. Anyway, he was prepared to arrest me for the murder of my husband Glenn on the merest suspicion, and that loathsome reporter wasn't any better. Of course the buffoons didn't even realize that Glenn was still very much alive. It was most disgusting. The only reasonable person present that day was you, Max. You helped them see the light of reason and corralled them away quickly. I was very grateful."

Max fought the urge to remind her that she did not act very grateful at the time, and simply said. "I'm just glad it worked out. Of course, your husband showing up had a strong effect too."

"At any rate, Max. I am grateful, and since that time I have regarded you as a competent and reasonable man. Of course, being married to Allison is proof of that as well."

"That's what I keep telling him," said Allison, raising her glass in salute.

"So I am asking you to consider our position here and continue your efforts to keep certain people from getting carried away; people such as newspaper reporters."

"Mrs. Stilwell, I have no control over the press. Besides, when a murder occurs, publicity follows. I don't see how you can avoid it."

She shook her head. "I imagine that friend of yours at the Star-Democrat will be pestering you for inside information, if he hasn't already."

"Chip Carswell? No, he won't, because he knows he won't get it," said Max. "If you know anything about me at all, Mrs. Stilwell, you know I am not a publicity seeker, but the Stilwell Building will be a magnet for the press regardless of whatever I do."

"I told my husband Glenn that buying that building was a mistake," Mrs. Stilwell grumbled. "I've been against it from the beginning. Buying a public building and putting our name on it was just asking for trouble. It'll just make us a target, I said. It just isn't fair, but once Glenn gets an idea in his head nothing can dissuade him."

"But any building would be mentioned in the press under these circumstances," Allison reminded her.

Gunther, the estate manager jumped in. "That's true enough, but when people are as well-known as the Stilwells the papers give such a story extra attention and keep it going longer. The Stilwells don't expect to be exempt from attention, but they don't feel it's fair that they should be raked over the public coals simply because of their position. It'll just encourage people to file lawsuits in hope of an easy payday."

"Look," said Max, with a hint of testiness in his voice, "there's no getting around the fact that a man was murdered in that building. People tend to notice things like that and they talk about it. It's human nature, especially when it's in a locked room. I will be considered and discrete, but can't change any of that."

"I understand, Mr. Hurlock," said Mrs. Stilwell, dropping the less formal "Max." "And that brings us to the second point I would like to suggest that you consider. Why was the room locked?"

Max shrugged. "I don't know yet. Killers stage murders that way for several reasons. Maybe they want it to look like suicide, or maybe they want to challenge the police, or maybe they want to make murder harder to prove..."

"Or maybe," Gunther interjected, "they wanted to embarrass the Stilwells!"

Allison almost choked on a piece of beef Wellington when she heard this. "Do you mean to suggest that the murder was committed simply to give the Stilwells a black eye?"

"Not the murder; of course not," Mrs. Stilwell replied, taking over for Gunther once again. "But isn't it possible that, having committed the murder, the killer also wished to generate maximum bad publicity for us? Even at the Stilwell Building, people's interest in an ordinary murder would be quite short-lived, but a murder in a locked room in the Stilwell Building? They will be talking about *that* for years."

Ned Gunther chimed in. "We're not saying that was the purpose of the murder. I'm sure there was some powerful motive we haven't discovered yet, but maybe the killer also had some sort of grudge against the Stilwells and wanted to gain the maximum bad publicity for them"

Max nodded. "That's an interesting point, and one I admit hadn't occurred to me. I will keep it in mind as a possibility. Of course, that makes finding the killer even more complicated. It would have to be someone with a motive against both the victim *and* the Stilwells. I don't suppose you know of anyone like that?"

But both Jacqueline Stilwell and Ned Gunther remained silent, staring at their Beef Wellington.

"How about any of the current tenants of the Stilwell Building?" Max asked. "Do any of them harbor ill feelings towards the Stilwells?"

"I understand that Grayson Dunlop has been complaining about his rent increase, but it's just grumbling. I'm not aware of any real problems in that regard."

"Doesn't mean a thing," Gunther grumbled. "We can't name anyone who was angry at Leroux, either, but he's dead just the same."

## Chapter 9
## Suspects

The next day dawned cooler and Max headed back to Easton after dropping Allison off in St Michaels to interview the manager of the packing house. The packing house was at Navy Point, and consisted of several wooden barn-like buildings alongside a story-tall pile of empty oyster shells. The owner Nat Conway, had an office off one of the loading docks by the railroad tracks. Allison stepped over the foul smelling puddles and knocked on the bare wood door.

"Yeah. Come on in!" someone yelled from inside. She pushed open the door to reveal a dingy room with a desk, a few chairs, some filing cabinets, and some clipboards. Behind the desk and the solitary telephone sat the owner, a hulking man with short brown hair who looked to be in his 30s. He wore a shirt with the tie loosened.

"Mr. Conway?"

"Yeah; that's me. I guess you're Allison. Sit down, Toots."

"You can call me Mrs. Hurlock. Thanks for seeing me. I'm researching an article on the new bridge across the bay they're talking about and I wanted to get your point of view. Do you think a bridge would help your business here at the packing house?"

93

Conway leaned back in a thoughtful pose and looked at her critically. "You look a little young to be writing about the packing business."

"You look a little young to be *running* a packing business," she replied, "so maybe we should respect each other's opinions."

Conway smiled. "Pardon me. Now what was that you wanted...oh, yeah. The bridge. Well, Toot...er Mrs. Hurlock, I could sell directly to Baltimore and ship from there if they built a bridge. Now I got all the business I can handle already, but it all goes north to Wilmington cause that's where the rail goes. It's the only game in town. But if Baltimore was handier, I could maybe get those boys bidding against each other and fetch a better price for crabs and oysters."

"So a bridge would be good for you?"

"Not just me. The shore is covered with small packing houses packing and shipping oysters, crab meat, and tomatoes. A bridge would help all of 'em."

"So you'd be all for it?"

"For the business, yes, but I don't know what would happen if the shore suddenly became easy to get to. I figure we'd maybe have a flood of out of towners cloggin' up the roads, drivin' up land prices, and maybe makin' it hard for me to hire pickers."

"What do you mean?" said Allison.

"I employ several hundred people here, shuckin' oysters, and pickin' crabs, It's all piece work. They all get paid by how much they pick or shuck or pack. It doesn't pay a lot, but it's a way for folks to get by. It's one of the few places a colored can walk right in the door and get a job. Of course, I got lots of whites workin' here, too. Some of the women bring their small kids and let them help out. If I had to compete with a bunch of Western Shore people over here employing the same people buildin' houses or startin' businesses, or even hiring domestic help, I might be in trouble. I'd have to pay more to get people to work here and raise prices to cover it. I don't know if the Baltimore market would be enough to make up the difference if that happens."

"I see. You've given this a lot of thought."

"All I can tell you, Mrs. Hurlock, is that the question is a lot more complicated than folks realize. Some people will get rich but some people will get hurt."

As Max approached police headquarters, he heard a familiar voice.

"Hey, Max! Wait up."

Max turned. "Chip Carswell, ace reporter. What brings you here, as if I didn't know."

"What else? The Bucket Shop Murder."

"Is that what they're calling it?"

"Has a nice ring to it, doesn't it? So I understand they have you involved in it. That's a good move on their part. They know you can sleuth rings around them."

"I think the fact that I don't run my mouth is more important."

"So what do you think? I understand the police have several jilted women and swindled investors on the suspect list. And what connection do the Stilwells have to this?"

Max raised his eyebrows. "Didn't you get your fill of falsely accusing the Stilwells last time?"

"I'm not accusing anyone," Carswell shot back. "That's your department. I'm just digging for the facts. Being a reporter means asking questions."

"Sure; and being discrete means not answering them. I'll see you later, Chip."

"Wait, Max. What about the missing lease?"

"The what?"

"I hear they can't find the lease that Leroux signed when he moved in. Pretty strange, wouldn't you say?"

"I have to go," Max said.

Chief Vickers was also anxious to talk to Max. "Max; you're just in time. we found Harold Santino and brought him in. Care to sit in on the interrogation?"

"Sure. Which way?"

The Easton Police headquarters was in a small building with several jail cells attached. There was no big city interrogation room, just an all-purpose room where the staff ate lunch. Max and the chief sat on one side of the table and saw a surprisingly sour-looking man with wire rimmed glasses and a scraggly brown beard on the other. The chief started the questioning.

"Mr. Santino, I understand you patronized Chesapeake Investments."

He shrugged and examined his fingernails. "It's no secret. I thought it was a proper stockbroker, but found out he was no better than a bookie."

"What do you mean?"

Santino looked up from his fingernails. His tight-lipped expression still looked as if he'd been sucking on a lemon. "He took my money for Howell Company stock, and told me it went down to less than half in a month. I have a small family farm. I can't afford to roll the dice. I need a stable investment. All I asked was to get my money back. He took it under false pretenses!"

"What do you mean?" Max asked.

"He had all these fancy charts and that big slate board on the wall, and told me about how much money his other clients made. Pretended he was an expert, but never said a word when I selected the stock. Turns out they had a merger deal in the works and it fell through. Then the week after, the top guy was arrested. There's no way Leroux didn't know that was coming. He played me for a sucker and I just wanted my money returned."

"So I guess you were pretty angry at him," the chief suggested.

"Of course I was. I was counting on that money." Santino folded his arms and slumped in the chair defiantly. "I asked him nicely, and he just said I had bad luck. Bad luck! I came back several times and, yes, I guess I did get a little irate with him, but he wouldn't budge."

"Where were you the night before last?" the chief asked.

Santino started and sat up. "I was home on the farm, trying to figure out how to make ends meet...as usual."

"And did anybody..."

"Well, I had Pat Cassidy the plumber come by and give me an estimate on a new well pump, but that was around seven or so. I ain't got an alibi for nine o'clock if that's what you're driving at, but I didn't kill Leroux. I would never do that, you danged fool; can't you see? As far as I'm concerned, Leroux getting killed is the worst thing that could have happened."

"How's that?"

"Now I'll never get my money back."

After some more equally unproductive questioning, Santino was dismissed. Chief Vickers sighed and looked at Max.

"Well, what do you think of Mr. Santino, Max? Did he kill Leroux?"

"Unlikely, but not impossible," said Max, leaning back in his chair. "As long as Leroux was around, there was a chance, however small, that Santino would recover some of his losses. That's a pretty strong incentive to wish for Leroux's continued good health. On the other hand, lashing out at someone who bilked you is a pretty strong incentive, too. The question is; which one was strongest for Harold Santino?"

"How about his alibi?"

Max shook his head. "Well, if Pat Cassidy the plumber came by at seven thirty and left by eight, Santino would have had plenty of time to get to Easton and kill Leroux."

"I guess you're right, Max. We'll just have to see. Oh, I meant to tell you; we checked out Leroux's place. He lived in a boarding house over on Goldsborough Street."

"So did you find anything interesting?" said Max.

"Well, it was funny. We never did find anything tangible that could shed light on the case, but the place was, well, strange."

"Strange?"

"Well, it's hard to explain, but the whole setup seemed temporary. He had three rooms, but seemed to be living out of a couple of steamer trunks. It looked like he was only there temporarily; like he was ready to clear out on a moment's notice. What do you suppose that could mean, Max?"

Max shook his head. "It could mean a lot of things....or it could mean nothing. We just don't have enough information yet."

"Chief, Mr. Stilwell is here," said an officer suddenly appearing in the doorway.

"Tell him...oh, there you are, Mr. Stilwell."

Glenn Stilwell filled the doorway and burst into the room. "All right, Vickers; what progress have you made?"

"We're going through the tenants and seeing who had what relation with Leroux. Max here is making some inquiries of his own."

"I ran into that Carswell guy outside snooping around. What did you tell him?"

"Actually, Mr. Stilwell," said Max, "he told us something. Is it true that Leroux's lease is missing?"

Stilwell looked startled, then indignant. "I don't see how that matters, but if you must know, yes. It's true. He was on a month to month lease and it seems to have gone missing, but I think it's a safe bet he wasn't murdered over a clause in his lease."

"No, I suppose not," said Max, "but it is a loose end and we have to look at everything related to the case."

"Right now," Vickers jumped in, "we are interviewing people and Max has been in touch with an art expert."

"Art expert?" Stilwell looked as if he couldn't take much more. "First a misplaced lease and now an art expert? You're just thrashing about in every direction. Max, if you weren't involved I'd go and hire a private detective right now. However, I'll be patient a little longer."

"Thanks you, Mr. Stilwell," said Vickers. "That's very..."

"But not forever!" With that parting shot, Stilwell was gone as abruptly as he had come.

The sudden silence was broken by another policeman sticking his head in the now-vacant doorway.

"Chief, there's a reporter from the Washington Post on the phone."

Vickers looked at Max. "I was afraid of this; so was Stilwell. I understand Glenn Stilwell was some kind of diplomatic liaison during the war, and the Stilwells were very big in Washington circles. That means this case is going to get a lot of unwelcome attention."

"Is there any other kind?" said Max.

The chief's conversation with the Washington Post reporter was brief. When it was over, the chief reappeared in the main room where Max was looking through the police reports.

"Well, that was quick," Max remarked.

"He's coming here tomorrow."

"Well, we'll just have to get it solved by then," said Max.

"When Glenn Stilwell sees his name splashed all over the Post in connection with a murder, I might be looking for a new job," said the chief gloomily.

Max nodded in sympathy. "Look, public relations are not my game, but it seems to me you are under no obligation to spill the beans to a reporter, especially about an ongoing case. Why don't you ask the mayor how he wants you to handle it."

Chief Vickers brightened up. "That's a good idea. He already told me to let him know what develops. I'll go see him right away. Meanwhile, maybe you could go and talk to Marsha Tolley for me and find out if she was having an affair with Leroux."

"What? She would never tell me."

"Come on, Max. I know you can be pretty smooth when you have to be. Please. I have to see the mayor but the case has to go forward. You'll be saving my hide."

"Again," said Max.

The crowd around the Stilwell building was gone except for the occasional passerby stopping to stare and to whisper. An officer stood guard outside Chesapeake Investments. Otherwise, all was quiet again.

Marsha Tolley was thirtyish and had hair much more red than nature would have provided without chemical assistance. She was stylishly dressed in a tweed suit in spite of the warm weather, and seemed delighted to see Max.

"Why, hello, Max. Where is that charming wife of yours today?"

"Being charming somewhere else at the moment. Chief Vickers asked me to have a little chat with you; just some routine things we have to account for. Is this a good time?"

"Well, it's too early for lunch," she replied. "Otherwise I might demand a meal as the price of my cooperation."

"Maybe some other time. I have a feeling I'll be around here more than once. So did you know Mr. Leroux well?"

"Look, Max," she sighed "I'm sure you already know we were...involved. He has a shrew of a wife who won't let go, and we were waiting to get married. Yes I was peeved at him, if you must know. I thought he should lay down the law and break free once and for all. We had a few knock down arguments about it and I admit I was pretty outraged at times, but I didn't kill him. I mean, come on; I can't very well marry a man if he's dead, can I?"

"Did he promise to marry you?"

"Not in so many words, but he did mention his wife and how they were separated but not yet divorced." She sighed. "Now that I look back on it, I should have known it was a bad bet."

"How's that?"

"Now that I look at it, he really lost interest in me several weeks ago. That's when I heard he was seeing someone else; someone named Violet."

"Violet who?"

"No idea, just some young thing named Violet. Anyway, he was chasing her and neglecting me, and after I helped him get his business going."

"Oh? How did you do that?"

"When he first came here, he didn't know anybody and he wanted to get some customers. He used to ask me where all the potential investors were around here. He figured I had a good handle on where all the big houses were and who lived in them, especially the waterfront mansions. I told him that those people already had stockbrokers, probably the big firms managing their accounts. He'd never be able to pry them away, but he was still interested."

Max nodded. "Did he ever talk about anyone who might be out to get him?"

She made a vague gesture. "Oh, he had his share of unhappy customers, but other than that Santino guy, none of them seemed really sore-not enough to kill him, anyway. Still, you never really know people, do you? I mean, for all I knew, he was mixed up in bootlegging and running illegal liquor at night. He wouldn't be the only one."

While he was at the Stilwell Building, Max decided to drop in on Grayson Dunlop and ask about the money he had lost with Leroux, but Dunlop was out somewhere, so he went into Leroux's office and took another look around. A bored patrolman was still on guard and gladly let Max in.

"Has anybody else been around trying to get in?" Max asked.

"A few," was the reply. "There was this fella from the Star-Democrat who offered me a sawbuck to let him get in and take pictures."

Chip Carswell, Max thought. "So what did you do?"

"I told him that there was evidence that couldn't be disturbed. It would be all my job is worth to let a reporter in to take pictures. They'd be in the paper the next day and the chief would want to know how they got there."

Max stepped into the office once again. The desk had been cleaned out and the contents boxed and taken to police headquarters as evidence. Max went to the rear window and inspected to brickwork. It did look like an amateur had been trying to fix it. Maybe it had nothing to do with the crime. He looked at the lock on the front door and found it was the old-fashioned kind that could be opened or closed with a skeleton key. Of course, that didn't explain how it got locked from the inside when the killer was presumably outside. He made a mental note to examine the key at police headquarters.

The clock at the courthouse was striking 12, so Max went back to police headquarters and found the chief had not yet returned from the mayor's office.

"I need to see the evidence boxes in the back room," he asked the receptionist.

"Sure thing, Mr. Hurlock. You know the way."

Max pulled out a box and found it filled with papers. In addition to business papers and receipts, he found two folders. On was marked "Stock slips found in top right drawer". The other was labelled "Stock slips found in bottom left drawer." He glanced at the slips and found them to be the same ones he had noticed earlier. A small envelope caught his eye.

It was labeled simply "Key".

Max opened the envelope and found a plain metal key, the kind a child might draw if he were asked to show what a key looks like; a center shaft with a head (called a bow) for turning on one end and the tab that engages the lock (called the bit) on the other. Max had learned the basics of keys a few years before when Allison was researching an article about magic tricks. There was nothing unusual about the key. Max held it to the light and turned it slowly.

"See anything, Mr. Hurlock?"

Max looked up and saw Officer Fred DeGrange grinning at him. "Hey, Fred. I'm just checking out the evidence once again. Did you notice this key?"

DeGrange squinted at the key. "Sure thing. I took it out of the lock myself...the *inside* of the lock."

"I suppose you noticed the scratches."

"Scratches? Where?"

"Right here on the end of the shaft. If the key was in the inside of the lock, the end of the shaft would have been facing towards the outside."

DeGrange squinted some more. "Well, I'll be. You're right, Mr. Hurlock. There's some tiny little scratches there. What do they mean?"

Max looked at the scratches. "I don't know. Maybe nothing. It's not unusual for a key to get scratched when someone fumbles to get it in the lock. You see it a lot with drunks, or people with bad eyesight or people who lack a steady hand."

He put the key back in the envelope. "Just one more loose end."

## Chapter 10

## The Fourth Estate

Allison got a lift back home with Iris Dalrymple, the town librarian and resident expert on nearly everything.

"A bridge across the bay? It'll never happen. The bigwigs in Wilmington and Philadelphia would never allow it." Iris was sure.

"Why would they care?"

"They don't want the competition! Right now, they have the whole Eastern Shore market in their pocket. If a bridge gets built, suddenly they'll have to compete with the Port of Baltimore."

"But how could they stop it?"

"Oh, they'll pretend it's a safety issue, or some such; anything but good old greed. They'll plant editorials and articles about how dangerous a bridge would be and how ships might crash into it. In the end, the bridge will get delayed to death. You'll see."

"Hmmm," said Allison. "I think I just got an angle for my article."

Max returned an hour later to find Allison typing on the front porch.

"Ah, so you've decided to do the bridge article?"

"Yes, Iris Dalrymple gave me a good angle; the political and economic interests clashing over the bridge."

"A little heavier than your usual articles, isn't it?"

"A little, but it's an important subject. Maybe it'll open people's eyes around here."

"Sounds great. You'll knock it out of the park."

Allison leaned back in the wicker chair and stretched. "So have you caught the murderer yet? You've had almost the entire day."

"Very funny. No, the layers of the onion are still being peeled back. Glenn Stilwell said he thought Leroux might have had some source of income nobody knew about. He thought it might be an inheritance or something, but I wondered if it could be rumrunning."

"Rumrunning?" Allison sat up in the chair. "That would explain not only the income, but possibly why someone would want to kill him. Could the murder be just a fight over territory? Maybe the whole bucket shop operation was just a front."

"Yes, it does open up some possibilities," said Max. "One thing's for sure; the case is getting more complicated. To make things worse, some Washington Post reporter is coming tomorrow. Once the articles start appearing, the Stilwells will be fit to be tied and the police will be so busy looking over their shoulders they'll never get anything done. Small towns weren't made for big murders."

Allison just shook her head and leaned back with her eyes closed.

Max did the same, and they sat on the porch draining away the cares of the day. Presently, Allison frowned.

"Max," she said, her eyes still closed, "do you hear a car?"

"Ignore it. Maybe it will go away."

"It's getting louder."

"Quiet; I'm busy ignoring it," said Max.

Allison opened her eyes. "It's a car all right and it's heading this way. That's how this whole mess started. Well, if there's been another murder, we're moving."

Max opened his eyes. "Two men. That looks like Chief Vickers and ...Jim Clark, the Mayor of Easton."

"What?"

The car pulled up and the two men got out. "Hello again, Max. Hello Allison," said Chief Vickers, tipping his hat. "You know Jim Clark?"

Max shook his hand. "We met once or twice. How are you?"

"I've been better," said the mayor. "That's what I came to see you and Miz Allison here."

They arranged themselves on the porch and the mayor spoke up. "First off, I appreciate the work you're both doing with this murder we got up in Easton. I'm confident you and the chief here could get to the bottom of it if only everybody else would stay out of it."

"A big if," said Max.

"You know we got lots of folks nipping at our heels and ready to scream blue murder anytime we slip up. It's like working in a fishbowl. I'm concerned the hoopla surrounding this case will hinder the investigation and give the entire Eastern Shore a black eye if we don't find a way to deal with it. So I came all the way down here to talk to you both directly because this is one place nobody'll be listening in."

"Sure, Mr. Mayor..."

"Jim."

"All right. Sure, Jim, but what can we do? After all, people have a right to ask questions; even reporters."

"Don't I know it? We already got your pal Chip Carswell sniffing around. Well there's a reporter from the Washington Post due here tomorrow, and more are sure to follow. Now, I'm not saying we should refuse to cooperate, but I'm afraid of what will happen if we do. My problem is I don't know how to handle these boys. If I say too much, it'll get splattered all over the papers and make me and the town look bad. If I don't say enough, they'll accuse me of hiding something. I'm just a small town mayor; I'm not good at this sort of thing. When a reporter asks me a question it usually involves a street project or a sewer line extension."

"I see the problem," said Max.

"I need someone to handle the press for me in this case, sort of a press secretary. I need someone who knows the news business and is good with words and how to say things properly without going hog wild. I need someone who has worked in the press and knows how they operate; someone who would have credibility with those people."

"Uh, oh," said Allison, under her breath. "A cannibal is about to invite me to lunch."

"I have discussed this matter at length with Chief Vickers and he assures me there is only one person for this job. So I'm here to ask in person if Miz Allison would be the official press secretary for the Town of Easton."

All eyes turned to Allison. "Me?"

"Who better?" said the mayor. "You're smart, you have experience with the press; you're good with words, and you're married to one of the chief investigators. And truth be told, even though I don't claim to be an expert on reporters, there's one thing I am sure of; they'd rather talk to an attractive woman than a crusty old Eastern Shore politician. So how about it? Would you be Easton's official press secretary?"

"With all due respect....Jim; do you realize how absurd that sounds?" said Allison. "A town of a few thousand people with an official press secretary? That's a good way to make Easton a laughing stock all over the East Coast."

The mayor turned to Vickers. "You were right about her, Tom. She's smart as a whip, and she has a pretty good feel for politics to boot. Even I didn't think of that."

He turned back to Allison. "But will you....that is, could you...."

"Relax," said Allison, taking charge of the bewildered faces around her front porch, "I'll do it, but I can't be an official anything or you'll get in trouble with the civil service rules, and sound pretentious in the bargain."

"Miz Allison," said the mayor, "I'll call you the Queen of the Nile if it'll get the press off my back. With your writing and press experience, you'll know just what to say, and more importantly, what *not* to say. Then it's settled. What do you think is the best way to proceed?"

Allison thought a moment. "I suggest you arrange a very busy out-of-town schedule for yourself for the next few weeks, but hold a quick press conference tomorrow afternoon with Chip Carswell and the Post reporter. In that conference you will express your desire to work closely with the press on this most important case, and that you have asked me to be a temporary liaison to make sure there is no delay getting information out, since you will not be available much. Then turn the floor over to me and I'll do the rest."

The mayor had the relieved look of a man who had thought he was going blind only to find that his hat was too big. "Yes...yes, that would be wonderful. By God, we just might get through this thing yet."

"When someone corners the chief," Allison continued, "he should say they are pursuing possible leads. If they pry into specifics, he can say he can't talk about the details of an ongoing investigation. Then I can give them just enough for a story, but not enough to compromise the investigation. Now, I'm working on an article and I may have to take a day trip to Philadelphia or Baltimore, but we'll just have to work around it. On those days, Jim, you will *not* be available."

The mayor was nodding rapidly. "Yes, yes, of course. Thank you Miz Allison. I feel better already."

"Oh, one bit of information that might be helpful, Chief Vickers," said Allison, "What is the clearance rate for murders in Easton and Talbot County?"

Chief Vickers looked as if someone had smacked him with a wet sock. "Clearance...oh, you mean how many were solved? Let's see. We had ten last year and solved eight of them. Of course, they were all drunken bar fights or domestic problems, nothing like this."

"Never mind. I'll need basic statistics on area covered, number of officers, and the like," said Allison. "It might come in handy if we get criticized for not moving quickly enough."

"I'll write it up and get it to you tomorrow," said Vickers, visibly relieved.

"While we're all here and out of the public eye, maybe we should summarize what we know so far," said Max. "We have two people. Grayson Dunlop and Harold Santino, who lost money with Leroux and were not happy about it. Neither one has an alibi for the night of the murder. We have Marsha Tolley, who was feeling cheated by Leroux because he wasn't pushing hard enough for a divorce, and because he was apparently seeing yet another woman we know only as Violet. Violet herself, whoever she is, may have a motive, but we haven't been able to track her down yet. Leroux's wife, who we also haven't been able to find yet, is apparently the vindictive type, so she might have had a motive as well. Glenn Stilwell doesn't have any obvious motive, but he says that he thinks Leroux had some independent source of income. That brings up the possibility of bootlegging and a murder over territory."

"And what about the locked door?" said the mayor. "How in the devil did they pull that off?"

"I have an idea about that," said Max, "but I think we should concentrate on the who rather than the how at this point. Once we locate Mrs. Leroux, she might be able to give us more background on Leroux's interests and contacts. What about the medical examiner? Do we have a report yet?"

"We'll have the formal report tomorrow," said Vickers. "Informally, the doctor told me there were two .32 caliber bullets found. One hit the heart and was instantly fatal. Powder residue was found on Leroux's sleeve, probably from a defensive gesture. No shell casings were found, so the gun was likely a revolver. There was nothing else unusual."

"The killer used .32 caliber bullets?" said Max. "That's a pretty small round. It might indicate that the killing wasn't premeditated. If the killer was planning to shoot Leroux before he arrived, I would have thought he'd bring something bigger to make sure."

"Maybe he just had it with him," said Vickers, "or maybe he grabbed Leroux's gun."

"I'm talking to Grayson Dunlop tomorrow," said Max. "I'll keep the small caliber in mind. Chief, if you could have your boys talk to some of the bootleggers around here, and don't tell me you don't know any, maybe we can find out if Leroux was mixed up in that."

After some more discussion, Chief Vickers and the mayor left with a lot of thanking and handshaking.

As the car disappeared down the lane, Max turned to Allison.

"Allison, no one has a higher regard for your abilities than I do, but how in the world are you going to keep that pack of press wolves at bay once this thing really gets rolling?"

"The Easton Police," replied Allison, in a businesslike voice, "assisted by other local law enforcement resources such as the Talbot County Sheriff's Office and a well-known local private investigator is currently investigating several avenues and narrowing down the possibilities in this case. They are also seeking several more persons of interest. They are making progress towards a conclusion, but in order not to compromise the investigation, they are not able to release any details at this time. Be assured, however, that any information whose confidentiality is not essential to the investigation will be shared with the press immediately. The Easton Police Department has a clearance rate for murders of eighty percent."

Max nodded his head. "I'm convinced; now if the newspaper boys swallow it, everything will be copacetic."

# Chapter 11
## Some gentlemen of the press

As he walked to police headquarters the next morning, Max read the headline of the Easton Star-Democrat and shook his head.

STOCKBROKER MURDERED IN EASTON

*Shot dead in locked room in Stilwell; Building*
*Real-life Eastern Shore mystery*

So much for working behind the scenes, he thought.

"Look, I told you everything I know, which isn't much. The guy was a glorified bookie and lots of people lost money with him. I was one of them. That's all I know." Grayson Dunlop sat in the interrogation/lunch room of Easton Police headquarters nervously smoking a cigarette. He wore an expensive-looking gray suit and sported slicked-back brown hair. Chief Vickers and Max sat on the other side of the table.

"His records show you lost over $3,000," said Max. "Didn't that bother you?"

"Are you kidding? Of course it did, but I got over it. If you look at the record, you'll see I haven't had any transactions with Chesapeake Investments for almost two months. It's over and done with. I'm older, wiser, and a little poorer now."

"Do you think he ran an honest operation?" Vickers asked.

Dunlop shrugged. "I don't know. In a way, it would be hard for him to cheat, seeing as how the stock prices are published in the papers. I mean, he couldn't claim a stock went down when the paper shows it went up. On the other hand, he could feed you phony stock tips to get you to buy dogs, then keep the difference when the stock took a dive. Then, of course, if you didn't have the cash and you bought on margin, he'd charge interest besides."

"Is that what happened to you?" Vickers asked.

"Three times. He had this so-called inside information. I couldn't prove it was phony, but I suspected it. After a couple of bad experiences, I got wise and bailed out."

"And on the night he was killed, you were where?"

"I left the office at five and went straight home. My wife will tell you the same thing."

"Did Leroux get along with the others in the building?"

"Well enough, I guess. How he got on with any individual tenant depended on just how much that tenant had lost in the market."

"One more thing," said Vickers, "do you know anyone named Violet who might have been seeing Leroux?"

"Violet?" Dunlop shook his head. "No, I don't know about any Violet, but I seem to recall Marsha Tolley yakking about someone named Violet about a week ago."

"What did she say?"

"I dunno. She goes on about so many things, I sort of turned her off."


When Dunlop was gone, Max rose and stretched. "I don't suppose we've located Violet yet?"

"Not yet. We've been checking the telephone book and town records. We turned up eight Violets so far, but none are between the ages of ten and fifty."

"How about Leroux's wife?"

"She lives in Philadelphia, but when the Philadelphia police knocked on her door, a neighbor said she left with several suitcases the night before the murder."

"Did the neighbor have any idea where she was going?"

"Nope."

"That would have given her plenty of time to get to Easton and do him in," Max remarked. "Well, I suppose we'll just have to ask her when we find her. Anything else I should know?"

"Yes, as a matter of fact," said Vickers. "We found another tenant that lost some money to Leroux, about $2,000 worth; a fellow named Will Purdum. He runs the local office for a company trying to build a bridge across the bay."

"Allison already met him," said Max. "She's doing a follow up interview this morning. Maybe she can find out more."

Allison knocked on the door of the Chesapeake Bridge Company and heard the man inside reply. When she opened the door Will Purdum looked up and his face brightened. At the same time, he shuffled some papers on his desk. Allison noticed he hastily slid one sheet under the other.

"Ah, Mrs. Hurlock; so good to see you again."

"I hope you don't mind a few more questions," said Allison, smiling.

"Of course not! Fire away."

"I was wondering about the possible opposition to a bridge across the bay by shipping interests in Philadelphia and Wilmington."

"Purdum's face fell. "Oh, well. Of course a project of this magnitude will have a far reaching effect, and certain interests in Philadelphia and Wilmington are understandably concerned. Our job is to assure them that the increased business will benefit everyone."

Allison nodded. "I suppose you have lobbyists at the state house."

"We're trying to get our case across, but it's really just getting started."

Allison stole a glance at the stack of papers Purdum had been looking at when she walked in. She thought she saw some numbers and the words "stock holdings."

"Will you be issuing company stock for this project?" Allison asked.

"No, I think it will be revenue bonds, but that's up in the air at the moment."

"Do you have any personal experience with stocks, Mr. Purdum?"

"Oh, some," he replied. "Nothing gigantic, but I do play the market occasionally."

"Then you must have known poor Mr. Leroux on the second floor."

Allison thought she saw a look of derision for a second. "Oh, well I met him once or twice. I gave him some business, since his location was so convenient. I'm afraid it didn't work out very well."

"You lost some money?" Allison asked, with sympathy in her voice.

"Just spilled milk. I learned to stay away from bucket shops, so it wasn't a total loss."

"Do you mean he cheated you?" said Allison.

"I didn't say that. Look; the man is dead and may God have mercy on his soul. Whatever his faults, it's too late to do anything about it now."

Allison looked at Purdum closely and was sure he was gritting his teeth.


Max met Allison for a quick lunch at a local drug store soda fountain. The specialty of the place was toasted cheese sandwiches washed down with Cliquot Club Ginger Ale.

"Any progress?" she asked, swirling her straw in her glass.

"Just more of the same from Dunlop," said Max. "He lost money, but had no hard feelings. Also, they still can't track down the mysterious Violet, or the elusive Mrs. Leroux. She took a powder the night before the murder and hasn't been seen since."

"The night before? Then she could have..."

"Very possibly."

"Goody; another suspect! Anyway, I talked to Will Purdum about the bridge again and it seems he lost money with Leroux also," said Allison. "He downplayed it, but I think he was really mad about it."

The toasted cheese sandwiches arrived with just the right amount of slightly burned cheese on top. Max took a bite and contemplated.

"So are you ready for your big press conference?"

She shrugged. "I suppose so. We'll just have to see."

"Are you concerned?"

"Only that the mayor and Chief Vickers might ham it up for the spotlight and say the wrong thing."

"If they have any sense, they're keep as mum as possible."

"As I said, we'll see."


Meanwhile, a little over a hundred miles to the north, in front of a row of brown brick row houses on Rittner Street in South Philadelphia, Patrolman Frank Alberto was starting his second year on the Philadelphia Police force, but he was far from happy about it.

"Two years on the force, and what am I doing? I'm staking out an empty house in case this Leroux dame comes home. Nuts to this. They could have gotten a boy scout to do it."

He strolled to the corner twirling his nightstick in a way he hoped was authoritative. "I get to chase numbers runners and small time crooks; maybe the occasional bootlegger moving stuff across the river to Jersey if the state boys don't get him first. Sometimes, if I'm lucky, I get to break up a bar fight and actually arrest someone. Just small potatoes. If I just had a chance at a real big case, I'd show 'em what I could do. I guess this is as close as I'm going to get."

It was getting embarrassing. He walked the same tight beat up and down the same block keeping the same house under surveillance. The house stood empty, its windows dark and with no sign of life. The upper floor windows were like eyes looking down smugly at his helplessness. The front door remained stubbornly closed to the outside world.

At first, people in the neighborhood noticed him walking up and down, but now they were ignoring him, which was worse. "Three more hours in my shift. I wonder if I'd get some sort of commendation if I died of boredom in the line of duty?"

He stopped. A green car had pulled up in front of the Leroux house. Alberto watched, hardly daring to hope. A middle-aged woman matching Marie Leroux's description got out and went in the front door. Alberto smiled.

"Well, well, well. Looks like Mrs. Leroux is back from Maryland," he said as he turned and started back down the street. "She probably came home to wash the blood off her clothes after killing her husband." He slipped his nightstick into its ring and straightened his uniform. "Now we'll see who can crack cases around here."

The Mayor of Easton had called an "informal press conference" for two o'clock. Only two people showed up. Chip Carson recognized Al White, the Washington Post reporter as soon as he entered the mayor's office. White had been assigned to Eastern Shore stories on those rare occasions when they were covered by the Washington paper, and had run into Carswell several times.

"Al White," said Chip Carswell, "I see they sent you across the bay once again. You finally found a story worthy of your attention?"

White looked at Carswell the way a gorilla would look at a chimpanzee. "Chip Carswell; I see you're still covering stories about chicken farmers and backwoods moonshiners. In answer to your question, though, even you must have recognized that this story has some pretty juicy elements; a murder in a locked room, a building owned by a mysterious and reclusive millionaire living in a guarded mansion, and a bunch of small-town flatfoots trying to make sense of it all."

"And that's your angle?"

"Unless I get a better one. Look, Stilwell is a big noise in D.C. He was on the French Embassy staff during the war. Rumor has it he used to advise General Pershing. When a guy like that gets in trouble, it's big news."

"Who says he's in trouble?" said Carswell.

"That's what I'm here to find out," said White, dramatically opening the door to the mayor's office.

The mayor, Chief Vickers, and Allison were seated at a long table, in the conference room. Carswell and White sat opposite and spread out their notebooks. Introductions were made and White looked curiously at Allison, before turning to the mayor.

"Now, mayor, what I want to ask you..."

The mayor held up his hand. "I have a brief statement to make, then I'll turn the meeting over to Mrs. Hurlock."

"A dame?" White muttered.

"We have had a tragic death in Easton, one that presents a difficult challenge to law enforcement. The Easton Police under Chief Vickers here is working to solve this case and bring the guilty to justice. Because of the complexity of the case, and the necessity to cover every lead in a way that does not jeopardize the evidence, I have asked Mrs. Hurlock here to coordinate all updates and press information. Mrs. Hurlock lives in nearby St Michaels and is a former reporter for the Baltimore Sun. I have given her an important task; to obtain and provide you boys in the press with all information that we can safely release without hampering our efforts. If we do not release or comment on any specific matter, it will be to protect the admissibility or utility of the rest of the evidence. After all, catching the killer is only the start. We have to be able to convict him. So I'm going to turn the meeting over to Mrs. Hurlock and she'll fill you in further."

"Mayor, does this mean..."

"Thank you, Mr. Mayor," said Allison, ignoring White's half-formed question. "This is what we know so far. The victim is Charles Leroux of Chesapeake Investments in Easton. His body was found Tuesday morning in his locked office at the Stilwell Building near the courthouse. He was shot two times. No weapon or shell casings were found. The Easton Police are in charge of the case, assisted by the Talbot County Sheriff, the Maryland State Police, and various other cooperating agencies, as well as a local private investigator. They are gathering evidence and questioning witnesses at the present time. We will update you when we have anything else to report."

"Mayor, can you give us the names..." White looked from the mayor to the chief, then back again and got no response.

"We are still questioning witnesses and are bound to protect their identities at this stage," Allison said, as if the question had been addressed to her. Then she smiled. "I'm sure you understand the need for confidential sources. People speak more freely that way."

White hesitated a minute, then turned to Allison. "So is Mr. Stilwell involved in this?"

Allison smiled again. "As owner of the building and a good citizen, Mr. Stilwell is following the case closely. He has offered to cooperate in any way he can."

White looked at the mayor and Chief Vickers one last time, then sighed and turned back to Allison. "All right, honey. I guess I have to talk to you. What's your name again?"

"Allison Hurlock. Mrs. Allison Hurlock."

"All right. I suppose you're going to feed us the official approved information?"

"As the mayor said, I will tell you everything I can short of compromising the investigation or the evidence."

"Yeah, yeah. Well maybe you can tell me when an arrest will be made?"

"Certainly; just as soon as I know."

"Hmmm. And just who is this private investigator you mentioned. The one who's helping out?"

"Maxwell Hurlock."

White's eyebrows raised. "Hurlock? Is he..."

"My husband."

White made a note. "Nice cozy town you got here. Is the mayor your cousin, too?"

Allison was still smiling. "No relation. Neither is Chief Vickers."

"So what's so special about Hurl... your husband?"

"Max has had some experience with several other murder cases and the chief thought it wouldn't hurt to have his opinion...strictly informally you understand."

"What can you tell me about the Stilwells?"

"They are cooperating fully, but out of respect for their privacy, that's all I can tell you right now."

White snapped his notebook shut. "Great. Just great," he said, with sarcasm in his tone. "A flood of valuable information. I'd have done better with a phone call." He rose and walked out the door. Carswell watched him go and turned to Allison. "Well played, Allison."

The mayor and Chief Vickers just sat smiling, but Allison's smile faded. "He's not giving up that easily."

"Neither am I" said Carswell. "I have a few questions of my own."

In the outer office, the phone rang. A few seconds later, a secretary appeared.

"I'm sorry to interrupt, but the officer on the phone said it was important; something about Mrs. Leroux."

"What about Mrs. Leroux?"

"They've found her."

"Well, well," said Chip Carswell, "It seems my esteemed press colleague left a bit too soon."

Allison turned to Carswell. "I'm sorry, Chip, but you'd better give these gentlemen some privacy until they know just what the full story is."

"Aw, come on, Allison..."

"You heard me, Chip. I'll fill you in as soon as I can. Maybe you'll still scoop your pal Mr. White."

Carswell reluctantly left the office and waited outside anxiously, as Chief Vickers picked up the phone.

"Yes; this is Chief Vickers....yes...When was this? Just a little while ago? ..I see... Did she say anything else?...Where is she now?...If we sent someone up there would she answer a few questions?...All right; I understand ...Thank you."

Vickers replaced the phone and exhaled at the same time. "Can you beat that? She was visiting her mother who doesn't have a radio or a newspaper subscription. Or so she says. She claims she just found out and came home right away." Vickers sat shaking his head in frustration.

"So what happened? What did she say about her husband?" Allison asked.

"Nothing."

"What?"

"Apparently the Philadelphia Police patrolman who was staking out the place, a fellow named Alberto, got a little overanxious. Instead of just letting his sergeant know Mrs. Leroux was there, he barged in and started grilling her himself. He all but accused her of killing her husband to try to rattle a confession out of her."

"I take it that strategy was unsuccessful?" said Allison.

"And how. Instead of confessing, she clammed up and refused to talk without her lawyer. She didn't tell them a thing. What's more, her lawyer is a local barracuda who always advises his clients to keep their mouth shut. His motto is 'If the police want to convict you, why help them?'. I'm afraid we won't be getting much out of Mrs. Leroux."

"And if she did do it," said Allison, "it'll be hard to prove."

"But wasn't she an important witness?" said the mayor.

"Of course," said Vickers. "She would know why her husband came to Easton and whether he had any enemies, or if he felt threatened. She has the only inside information in the case. Now, thanks to an overbearing and overanxious patrolman, it's out of our reach."

*John Reisinger*

## Chapter 12

## Dead ends

The headlines the next morning were dramatic.

FEW CLUES IN BUCKET SHOP MURDERS

*Police and local investigator question other tenants*

*Authorities eye wealthy local mystery couple*

Despite the somewhat sensational headline, the story was accurate in recounting the case so far. Max, to his relief, was not mentioned by name, and neither were the Stilwells.

Max wasn't yet aware of the dramatic development with the reappearance of Mrs. Leroux. He had stopped by the Chesapeake Bridge Company to talk with Will Purdum. As a fellow engineer, Max hoped he could find out more about Purdum's apparent grudge against Leroux.

After discussing the engineering aspects of the bridge, a topic Max enjoyed very much, Max guided the conversation around to the late Mr. Leroux.

"Terrible thing about Mr. Leroux," Max stated flatly.

"Yes. Terrible," Purdum agreed, without much enthusiasm.

"Were you here when it happened?" Max asked. He knew no one else was in the building, but was trying to feel around for whether or not Purdum had an alibi.

"I wasn't in the office at all that day," was the reply. "I had to be in Rock Hall to meet with the mayor about possible sites for the bridge. I didn't get back until late. It was quite a shock when I came in the next morning, I can tell you."

"Well," said Max, "I suppose everyone was shocked. Charles Leroux didn't seem like the type to have lots of enemies."

No reply.

"Still, I expect he had his share of unsatisfied customers."

No reply.

"A lot of people lost money at his bucket shop, I understand, but I suppose it was their own fault."

There was a silent pause, then Purdum muttered. "Not necessarily."

"What do you mean?"

"I mean that Mr. Leroux did not always give accurate information to his customers."

"Not accurate?"

"Mr. Leroux was well known for his 'inside information', and some people put their money down based on that information. Then, when the information proved false, it was too late."

"Do you know this first-hand?" Max asked carefully.

Purdum was quiet a moment, as if trying to decide how much to reveal. Finally, he spoke. "I'm afraid I do. I bought quite a large amount, well, large for me, of Alleghany Consolidated Coal. Mr. Leroux told me he had heard that the company was about to be bought out by a much larger company that would buy back the outstanding shares at a hefty markup. He said that based on this upcoming development, he had to charge a premium on the certificates he sold me. I remembered reading something about some consolidation in the coal fields, so it seemed to make sense."

"So you bought some share certificates at a markup?" Max asked.

"The markup was higher than the share price at the moment, but less than the share price would become once the merger and buyback took place, so it seemed like a good investment. It wasn't. The merger never took place and I was stuck with shares I bought at the inflated price."

"Did you complain?"

"I was going to, but well,..."

"Well what?"

"Some other unhappy customer got there first."

Max made a mental note to check out Purdum's alibi carefully.


After Max left Purdum, he started towards city hall to see how the press conference had gone. As Max passed the courthouse, he heard a familiar voice behind him.

"I say Mr. Hurlock. What ho!"

Max turned and saw the rotund form of Nigel Smythe-Cunningham catching up to him.

"Quite jolly running into you again, Mr. Hurlock. I've been so wondering how that case of yours is progressing. Any more mysterious artwork involved that I could help with?"

Max shook his head. "I'm afraid not. It seems you were right about that book. It has nothing to do with the case, apparently."

Smythe-Cunningham looked disappointed. "Oh, I do call that hard. I was so hoping I could help out in some small way. A real-life mystery to solve, don't you know? Still, I wouldn't get all down in the dumps about that art book. It's rather like *Murder at the Crooked Horseshoe* by E. Whiting."

"I'm not sure I follow you," said Max.

"Well, in that story, the detective found a journal kept by the victim, but it was all written in code. Naturally, the detective assumed the journal had the key to the murder and much of the book was about his efforts to break the code, so to speak. Well, about halfway through the book, the bally code was cracked and they were finally able to read the entire journal."

"And...?"

"Well, that's what I'm driving at, you see. The journal was dull as dishwater. The poor chap recorded everything he did, no matter how prosaic. There was an entire page on washing his socks, for heavens sakes. The journal was just a red herring. It had nothing to do with the case. Your art book seems to have turned out the same way. I'm sorry for my sake, since I wanted to participate, but at least you eliminated what could have been a time consuming distraction. I expect the poor fellow simply ran afoul of one of his clients, or more likely, one of their wives. Still, that's life, what?"

"I suppose so. Well, thanks for the pep talk. Are you still leaving tomorrow?"

"Rather! I have finished appraising the estate I was called down here for and have made several acquisitions for my gallery in New York. I shall be checking out around noon. If I don't see you again, Mr. Hurlock, it has been a pleasure."

"Likewise."

"Cheerio!"


When Max walked into city hall, he found Allison talking to Chip Carswell.

"Hey, Max," Chip said. "Have you heard the news? Allison was just telling me. The Philadelphia police found Mrs. Leroux, but she isn't talking."

Allison nodded. "She returned home a couple of hours ago, but so far, she has nothing to say."

Max sensed there was more to the story, and changed the subject. Carswell, anxious to write his story, excused himself and left. When he was gone, Allison told Max the rest of the story.

"Of all the luck!" said Max. "We find the best lead yet and some over-eager flatfoot blows it for us. Well. It can't be helped now, I guess. We'll just have to hope either she changes her mind or we get the information we need somewhere else."

Allison thought a moment. "Maybe I could talk to her. You know; woman to woman. Maybe she'd open up a little."

Max shook his head. "Allison, I have great respect for your powers of persuasion, though I notice they seem to work better on men, but this isn't a whim on her part. She has a lawyer riding herd on her now, so I doubt you'd even get near her. I think you should await further developments before you head off to the City of Brotherly Love."

Allison sat back in the chair and sighed. "I suppose you're right. We'll just have to see what happens."

"At the moment, I'm afraid we're not making much progress. Pretty soon the newspapers will be noticing."

He picked up a newspaper lying on a nearby desk and started turning the pages. "Well, we're not on the front page at least. The big story is the voyage of the airship Norge and its attempt to cross the North Pole. It seems to have pushed everything else off the front page. Ah, here's an article on page four. 'STOCKBROKER MURDER IN EASTON: Local man found dead in locked room.' Hmmm. This is pretty basic, but I imagine they'll expand as they find out more."

A secretary appeared behind Allison. "Excuse me. Mrs. Hurlock? The mayor says there's a phone call for you."

Allison nodded and walked over to the telephone. "Who is it? Did he say?"

"Yes, Ma'am. It's Mr. Stilwell."

"Oh, great. Hello?"

"The mayor says you're handling the press," came the gruff voice on the phone. It sounded less like a question and more like an accusation.

"In a manner of speaking," she replied.

"Then maybe you can tell me what a Washington Post reporter is doing camping out by my gatehouse demanding an interview? I'm a prisoner in my own home!"

Allison grimaced. "That would be Al White. Apparently he wasn't satisfied with the information I gave him."

"Well make him leave!"

"I'm sorry, Mr. Stilwell, but we do have freedom of the press in this country. Putting reporters in jail is considered bad form, but you have freedom as well; you don't have to talk to him."

"But he's grilling my security people about my comings and goings. He says the public has a right to know."

"That doesn't mean you have an obligation to tell them, Mr. Stilwell. You'll just have to keep mum and he'll go bother someone else; probably me."

"All right, but you tell Max he'd better solve this case before things get out of hand!"

The line went dead.

"Al White, the Post reporter, is laying siege to Casa Leone and the lord of the manor is displeased."

Max chuckled. "I'll bet, and Jacqueline won't be far behind."

"When Chip Carswell's article comes out tomorrow announcing the locating of Mrs. Leroux, White will be fit to be tied."

"Chip will be on a cloud," said Max. "It's not every day he gets to scoop the Washington Post. Well, I think we can call it a day and head back to St Michaels before someone else takes exception to how we're doing."

A few minutes later, they were on the way down the St Michaels Road out of town.

"Max, don't you wish for a little obscurity sometimes? If you could work behind the scenes the way you have in other cases, you could get more done."

"I guess that's true, but I didn't pick either the case or the circumstances. We'll just have to tune out the noise and slog along."

"You're mixing metaphors again."

"It's been a long day."

They had a slow dinner of leftover pork chops, lightly burned, along with some boiled cabbage with vinegar. For desert, Allison had bought some cupcakes in town.

"So how is the baby coming along?" Max asked, as he chewed on a cupcake. "I hope all this confusion isn't upsetting him."

"Her. And everything is fine. Don't worry about the baby. At this stage, I'm the one doing all the work."

"Good. If it gets too much for you, let me know. I'll tell the mayor to get another press handler, or whatever he's calling you."

"I'm fine. It's like being in the news business again."

"Except that now, instead of being in the business of finding news, you're constricting it."

"Well, yes, but in a good cause. If we blabbed everything the minute we know it, no one would cooperate with the police and the case would never get solved."

Max leaned back in the chair. "Well, let's hope things clarify a bit real soon. A lot of people are watching."

Allison frowned. "Max, did you ever think of the possibility that Jacqueline Stilwell might have something to do with this?"

"Jacqueline Stilwell?"

"I know it sounds crazy, but she was against the Stilwell Building from the beginning, and as near as I can tell, her property manager, Nick Gunther was as well. Is it possible they staged the whole thing to discredit Glenn Stilwell and make him get rid of the building?"

"Allison, there is a long distance between not liking a building and murdering someone to get rid of it."

"Yes, of course, but suppose there was something else going on that made getting rid of Leroux desirable from her point of view? He pursued the ladies, apparently. What if he was making advances towards Jacqueline Stilwell? Or what if he was using the Stilwell's name to lend legitimacy to his insider stock tips? If he was some sort of threat to the Stilwells, he could have been targeted by Jacqueline, Glenn, or even the property manager, Ned Gunther. Don't forget, the Stilwells have always been a bit paranoid about outside threats. That's why they have the fence, the security guards, and the roaming Irish Wolfhounds at Casa Leone."

Max looked at her. "Whew! You have a devious mind."

"Yes, well we might be dealing with devious people."


The next morning, Max and Allison were just finishing breakfast when the phone in the hall rang. Max pushed off from the kitchen table and went to answer.

"If it's another murder," said Allison, clearing away the dishes, "tell them we're busy."

"Hello."

"Max. Tom Vickers here. You have to get in here right away."

"Sure. I'm just leaving anyway. What's up?"

"We found Violet."

# Chapter 13
# Violet

A young woman in her late twenties sat nervously in a chair in the makeshift interview room at the Easton Police headquarters. She wore a plaid dress with a fake fox fur collar and an imitation pearl necklace. She restlessly twisted a strand of her bobbed black hair.

"She called us this morning and we picked her up a few minutes ago," said Vickers. "She didn't even know we were looking for her, but she just wanted to get something off her chest. We couldn't find her because Violet is her middle name. She goes by it because her first name is Chastity. And are you ready for this, Max? She works as a maid at Casa Leone."

Max nodded. "Interesting. Let's go meet her."

Violet McGuinn looked up as the two men entered, Her eyes shifted from one to another.

"Hello, Violet. I'm Chief Vickers and this is Mr. Hurlock. Thank you for coming in and helping us."

Violet relaxed somewhat at the friendly tone, but kept twisting some strands of her hair. "I'm just doing my duty, sir."

"I remember seeing you at Casa Leone a few nights ago at dinner," said Max, smiling. "How are you?"

"Truth be told, I'm a bit nervous, Mr. Hurlock, but I came of my own accord."

"We appreciate it," said Vickers. "I understand you're the maid at Casa Leone?"

"That's right."

"And you were seeing Mr. Leroux off and on?"

"Yes, sir."

"How did you meet him?"

"Well, back several months ago, before Mr. Leroux started renting an office from Mr. Stilwell, Mr. Leroux contacted me. I work three days a week at the Stilwell house, and have an upstairs room in a boarding house on Hanson Street in town the rest of the time. Well, one day I find a letter from Mr. Leroux. Of course, I didn't know who he was, but the letter said he was trying to locate his cousin, Violet Mary McGuinn, and would like to meet me to discuss it. I wrote back saying I wasn't her, and he showed up at the boarding house one day with flowers to thank me for my trouble."

"Very generous," said the chief.

"Oh, I know. I should have given him the boot, but for a girl like me, it was an adventure, so we sat in the parlor and talked a bit. We hit it off and he offered to take me to dinner the next night. We started seeing each other after that."

"And he didn't have an office at the Stilwell building at that time?" Max asked.

"Not yet, no. Anyway, we went out for a few months, and one day he started talking about art. You know, paintings, and showing me a book he had with lots of paintings in it."

"Hold on a minute," said Max, leaving the room. "He was back in a minute with the art book.

"Is this the book?"

"Why yes, it is. Anyway, I didn't know anything about art and he sounded like an educated man, so we talked about the paintings in the book. He asked me if I'd noticed the paintings at Casa Leone and I said there were a few, but I didn't really take much note of them. Then he did something strange; at least, I thought it was strange. He showed me a painting in the book and asked me if I'd ever seen a painting like that at Casa Leone."

"He asked you about one specific painting in the book?"

"Yes, sir. I thought it was strange because the book had lots of other paintings but he was only interested in the one."

"Could you show us which painting?"

Violet thumbed through the color prints and stopped at one. "This one here."

Max and Vickers looked at the picture. It depicted an angel with a hand outstretched beckoning towards the viewer. The angel was glowing in a golden light and was smiling. The label simply said *The Smiling Angel of Reims*-Titian 1515.

"He asked if *this* painting was at Casa Leone?" Max asked incredulously.

"Not exactly, sir. He asked if they had anything that looked like it. He never said the original painting."

"And what did you tell him?"

"Well, sir, I told him I'd been in every room in the place many times, but I never seen anything like that. I was sure of it."

"So what happened?" said Vickers.

She shrugged. "Well, nothing really. He never asked again, but a few days later, he stopped calling on me as much. Then he stopped altogether. Then a few months after that, he was murdered, but I didn't have nothing to do with it, I swear!"

Max smiled. "Relax, Violet. Where were you the night of the murder? We have to check these things."

Violet looked ashen. "I...I was at Casa Leone. Mrs. Stilwell asked me to stay over to help serve at a dinner. I was there until past ten."

"And I assume the Stilwells were there as well?" said Max, making a note.

"Just Mrs. Stilwell. She was entertaining an old friend from Washington. Mr. Stilwell was out somewhere."

Max and Vickers looked at each other.

"So you never saw Mr. Stilwell that night?" asked Vickers.

"He did come back later, around ten-thirty or so."

Max excused himself, walked to the nearest telephone, and placed a call to the Avon Hotel. "You have a guest about to check out named Nigel Smythe-Cunningham. Would you please ask him to wait? Tell him Max Hurlock called and I need his art expertise after all. I'll be there in about fifteen minutes."

Allison stopped off at a local drug store for a phosphate before going to the library to look up statistics on the bay and the Eastern Shore economy for her article. She looked down at her stomach, but there was no sign of any baby-related changes yet.

She finished her drink and stepped out onto the street.

"Mrs. Hurlock!"

She had almost run into Al White. He was holding the morning Star-Democrat.

### VICTIM'S WIFE REFUSES TO TALK IN BUCKET SHOP MURDER

*Suspicions rise as Philadelphia Police confront Marie Leroux at home*

"Did you see this? This... rag that Carswell scribbles for scooped me on finding Mrs. Leroux. Is that how it's going to be? Are you going to be feeding information to the home town boy exclusively?"

Allison looked sympathetic. "I'm sorry it worked out that way, Mr. White. It was not intentional. The phone call came in just after you'd left, but while Chip Carswell was still there. You couldn't be reached since you were on your way to Casa Leone."

"Hurmph. And a fat lot of good *that* did me. The Stilwells are hermits. I sat there for hours. Even the guards wouldn't talk to me. So what else have I missed?"

"I'll have an update this afternoon at two and bring you up to the minute then."

"Hmmm. You're pretty slick for a small town girl. That mayor is pretty cagy getting you to handle the press."

"You have a job to do and so do I," said Allison, "and we all want the case solved."

"Fair enough. So what's your background, if I may ask? Are you from Easton?"

"Roland Park in Baltimore. Back in 1919, I wrote for the Sun under my maiden name, Allison Winslow."

White snapped his fingers. "Of course. I remember reading some of your stuff. It was pretty good."

"You should have seen it before the editors got hold of it."

Al White laughed heartily. "Ha! I have the same trouble. What they can do to a perfectly good English sentence is outrageous. But do you have some background in police work as well?"

"Max and I have been involved in several murder investigations, so despite my newspaper background, I think I have a pretty good idea of what information can or cannot show up on the front page."

"That's a pretty good background for this situation. Well, I'm an old newspaper dog myself; one of those ink-stained wretches. Trouble is, you get suspicious of everyone after a while. Well, at least we understand each other. I think when it comes to press secretaries, Mrs. Hurlock, you are about as good as they get."

"Why, thank you, Mr. White. That is the nicest compliment I've gotten all day."

White tipped his hat. "It's Al to a fellow reporter. See you at two."

Nigel Smythe-Cunningham was waiting in the lobby of the Avon Hotel when Max arrived.

"What ho, Mr. Hurlock! Such an unexpected pleasure. You have a need for my humble services?"

"Hello, Nigel. There's been a development. It seems our red herring may not be quite so red after all."

"I say; surely you can't mean that bally art book?"

"Got it in one, as you English like to say. It seems that Mr. Leroux was questioning one of the maids at Casa Leone about one of the paintings in the book."

"Questioning the maid? How extraordinary. What would she know about Renaissance painting, I wonder? Which painting was it?"

Max produced the book and opened it to the page. "This one."

Smythe-Cunningham's eyes lit up. "Oh, yes. The Smiling Angel of Reims. Exquisite. A remarkable work. She seems glow and reach out to you, doesn't she? This was from Titian's later period when he had more depth and intricacies in his color palate. Ah, what I wouldn't give to be able to offer something of this level in my gallery."

"What can you tell me about it?" said Max. "The book says almost nothing."

"Well, as I recall, it was purchased by the local bishop for the cathedral at Reims in France, back in 1520 or thereabouts, where it hung as the centerpiece in a special side chapel. A bit unusual for an angel to take center stage rather than a saint, but the painting as you can see, is magnificent. The cathedral at Reims, of course, is the traditional place where the kings of France were crowned. Charles the seventh was crowned there with Joan of Arc in attendance. It's one of the most sacred spots in the country. During the war, I understand that French soldiers used to pray to the painting for deliverance from battle wounds. Yes, the smiling angel is stunning; in a class by itself."

"So, is there any chance such a painting would somehow be hanging at the Casa Leone?"

Smythe-Cunningham laughed, his stomach rocking with the effort. "In Easton, Maryland? Oh no. my dear fellow; not the slightest chance. Absolutely none. There are few sure bets in this world, but this is one of them. The painting is not there. It is not even in the United States."

"You seem pretty sure."

"I am quite certain. My dear Max, didn't you know? This painting was destroyed in the war."

## Chapter 14

### Red herrings on canvas

Max sat stunned for a moment. "Destroyed?"

Smythe-Cunningham looked grim. "Oh, yes. The front was not far beyond the town of Reims and the Germans would shell the town off and on. They claimed they were not aiming for the cathedral, but hit it rather frequently nonetheless. The French are still reconstructing it, even now. Anyway, one shell hit the side chapel and either blasted or burned everything in it, including the angel; a bally war crime if you want my opinion. All they ever found was a charred corner of the frame."

You mean this book is a red herring after all?"

"The reddest, I'm afraid. It's like *The Second Venus* by Edward De Villiers. Everyone assumed an ancient statue has been stolen, when it had actually been destroyed by an earthquake. Oh, I assure you, dear fellow, I'm as disappointed as you are. I did so want use my art knowledge to help out in a real murder case. Mysteries are my passion, right after art itself, but I am quite certain our friend Mr. Leroux was not looking for *The Smiling Angel of Reims*. If he knew enough to know its value then he surely knew it was gone."

"Could he have been looking for a copy?"

"A copy? Why go to all that trouble for a copy? It's nonsense."

"Maybe he was looking for some other painting that was similar to the angel?"

"I jolly well doubt it," Smythe-Cunningham said, "because if such a painting had enough value to make pursuing it worthwhile, Leroux would easily have been able to procure a proper copy to show the maid. Art works of value are fairly well documented and cross-referenced. That, after all is my business."

"Then why would Leroux want the maid to look for a work of art that no longer exists? It doesn't make sense."

Smythe-Cunningham smiled wryly. "Actually, it might, under the circumstances. Perhaps I've been reading too much convoluted mystery fiction, but I wonder if Mr. Leroux simply picked the painting at random, not even knowing it had been destroyed, and used it to impress the maid with a knowledge of art he did not actually possess."

"You mean it was just a ploy to impress a woman?" said Max.

"Well, chaps have been known to blither all sorts of rot to impress the fair sex, wot? I mean to say, being an art connoisseur would sound more interesting to an impressionable young woman than being a cut rate stockbroker, I shouldn't wonder."

Max felt deflated. "Well, I asked for the truth and I got it. I appreciate your help. Sometimes things that appear to be one thing turn out to be something entirely different."

"Not to worry old chap," Smythe-Cunningham smiled, "That's the way I make my living. Very often I have to throw cold water on some fellow's hopes. A person will bring in some perfectly foul painting they found in an attic somewhere thinking it's a long lost masterpiece, but in most cases the canvas would have been put to better use patching someone's trousers."

Max smiled. "Well, if we have any more art-related questions, may I call you in New York?"

Nigel brightened up. "As it happens, you may not have to. I am not leaving just yet. I have been retained for another several days, possibly another week."

"Another estate?"

"Not a bit of it; the same one. It seems that Mr. Perryman's mania for collecting art gave his wife the pip and she didn't think a lot of it. A waste of good money, she called it. Anyway, to deceive his wife about the amount of art he was acquiring, Mr. Perryman kept a good bit of it in storage in a locked warehouse next to his factory. The executors just discovered the cache, and they contacted me yesterday for an appraisal. They believe there are well over a hundred paintings there, not to mention some very nice sculptures."

"Well, then I may be seeing you again. Thanks."

"Cheerio!"


When Allison walked into the conference room at police headquarters for the afternoon press briefing, she spotted a new face.

"Bob! Is that really you?"

"You two know each other?" Al White interrupted.

"Yes, ma'am. Bob Avery," said the newcomer. "You knew me as Bob on the Job back in your Sunpaper days. How are you Allison?"

"You're reporting state news for the Sunpaper now? I thought you were the sports guy for obscure teams."

"I've been promoted. I took your advice and stopped chasing the ladies long enough to concentrate on the work. Now here I am."

"Well, this is just great," grumbled Al White. "I'm the only one here who isn't an old pal of yours!"

"Well, welcome, Bob," said Allison. "I think we can get started. This is Bob Avery from the Baltimore Sun. Bob, this is Chip Carswell from the Easton Star-Democrat and Al White from the Washington Post. Since the briefing yesterday, the police have tracked down Mrs. Leroux up in Philadelphia. So far, unfortunately, Mrs. Leroux has declined to answer any questions or provide any information. In addition, a young woman who was seeing Mr. Leroux has come forward, but has not been able to throw any additional light on the case."

"Was that the mysterious Violet everyone was looking for?" Carswell asked.

"Yes," said Allison. "It turns out that Violet is her middle name, so she was harder to track for that reason. The police are still questioning her. Beyond that information, all I can tell you is that inquiries are proceeding."

"How does Glenn Stilwell fit into all this?" asked Al White.

"He owns the building where the murder took place and he is as anxious as anyone to see it solved," said Allison.

"Is he a suspect?"

"We have no suspect list as such. Inquiries are continuing and information is being evaluated and refined constantly."

"What about Grayson Dunlop's connection with local bootleggers?" Chip Carswell asked.

Allison felt a momentary rush of panic. This was completely new to her. Was Carswell bluffing, or were the police sitting on information and not telling her?

"Possible relationships and connections between individuals are part of the information that is currently being evaluated," Allison answered. "Beyond that, I have no information I can share at this time."

"But you don't deny that he's connected with bootleggers?" Al White took up the theme.

"Come on, guys; you know I can't talk about anything like that until we have something solid."

The press briefing broke up and Bob Avery was anxious to bring his former coworker at the Sunpaper up to date, so Chip Carswell slipped away before Allison could ask him where he got his information about Grayson Dunlop's supposed bootlegger connection. When the reporters were gone, she went directly to Chief Vickers's office.

"Tom, what's all this about Grayson Dunlop being connected to bootleggers?"

The chief looked up. "What? Who told you that?"

"Is it true?"

"This is the first I've heard. Sergeant!"

The sergeant on duty appeared. He knew nothing about any bootlegger connection either.

"We did bring in a bootlegger this morning," the sergeant volunteered. "A small-time guy from Port Street. He was making shine and selling it to some syndicate people."

"What did he have on him when arrested?" the chief asked.

"The usual stuff, a pack of cigarettes, house keys, a wallet, a small address book, some spare change..."

"Where is the stuff now?" Allison asked.

"It's in a box on my desk we haven't had a chance to list it yet."

"Could we look at the address book?" Allison asked.

The sergeant went and brought back a battered cardboard address book. Allison thumbed through the pages and saw Grayson Dunlop's name and phone number under D.

"Was Chip Carswell hanging around waiting for the press briefing when you brought the bootlegger in?" Allison asked.

"Uh, let's see. Yes, I think he was."

"Now we know what happened," said Vickers. "You left the items on your desk in plain view of the reporters and one of them, apparently Carswell, had a little peek."

"Look, chief," the sergeant flustered, "we got busy. We had the bootlegger, a drunk, and a couple of guys who were fighting on Washington Street. I just left the desk for a few minutes."

"How long do you think it takes to snoop in a notebook, sergeant?"

"Well..."

Vickers waved a hand. "Never mind. It's done. Just keep evidence away from prying eyes in the future."

"Yes, chief."

"Oh, and bring Grayson Dunlop in for questioning."

"Yes, chief."

When the sergeant had gone, Vickers turned to Allison. "This is why I have gray hair. So is Max coming by soon?"

"He said he was as soon as he talked to that art dealer about the picture in the book. Oh, here he is now."

Max walked in and the three exchanged notes.

"I have the sergeant bringing Grayson Dunlop in," said Vickers.

"Good," said Max, "but maybe we should have a chat with the bootlegger first. Then we can compare stories."

The bootlegger that awaited their attentions in the conference room was a weasely little man with thinning, slicked-down brown hair carefully combed to try to cover a bald area. A layer of stubble covered a receding chin. He was wearing overalls that badly needed washing.

"Hello, Calvin. I'm Chief Vickers. Seems we caught you driving a truckload of home brew towards Port Street. You planning on a little trip down the Tred Avon?"

The man shrugged. "Guess you got lucky."

"Maybe," said Vickers, "but you didn't. Now we can give you up to the Federal boys or maybe you can just get a little fine. That's up to the prosecutor, but your cooperation would help you a lot."

The bootlegger looked wary. "What do you want to know?"

Vickers motioned to Max to take over.

"We want to know about Grayson Dunlop," said Max in a casual tone. "Is he your backer, you bookkeeper, or what?"

The bootlegger let out a long sigh. "Well, I ain't admittin' nothing, mind you, but I'll tell you how things are. Makin' a living as a waterman is hard. Between the crabs and arsters you can't depend on and the way the prices go up and down, you can't hardly make ends meet. When Prohibition come along, suddenly there's an easy way to make money; running corn whisky across the bay. The Coast Guard and the feds were spread so thin, you hardly never got caught."

He paused, as if nostalgic for the good old days.

"But in the last few years, the enforcement's gotten tighter and only the fastest and biggest boats can make any money. That means most of the trade is controlled by syndicates. They got the money and the connections. So if a small guy wants to do business, he has to go through them. A small guy who makes good shine can sell it to the syndicates and let them worry about runnin' it. Now you can't just go lookin' for the syndicates. They like their privacy for obvious reasons. You got to go through a middle man to make the arrangements and handle the money."

"And that's where Grayson Dunlop comes in?" Max asked.

The bootlegger nodded. "When a man got some shine to sell, he contacts somebody like Grayson Dunlop. Dunlop contacts the syndicate and makes the arrangements. You call Dunlop and he tells you where to deliver it and pays you afterwards. That way, nobody can track anything back to the syndicate."

"How long has Dunlop been a middle man for the syndicate," Vickers asked.

"Couple years, far as I know."

Vickers shook his head. "You got a family?"

"Yes, sir. A wife and two kids."

"Sergeant, take him back and bring Dunlop in here, would you?"

When the man was gone, Max said "What's going to happen to him?"

"Him? Nothing."

"Not even a fine?"

"Hell, Max, a man like that hasn't got enough money to pay a fine. That's why he's doing this in the first place. No, I'll have a couple of the boys empty the bottles he was hauling. If anyone asks, I'll say it was a fire hazard. Then I'll give him a good tongue-lashing and let him go due to lack of evidence."

"Why, Tom," said Max. "You old softy, you."

"Max, I'm, just an old small-town cop. I don't know much, but one thing I do know; there's a lot of people who deserve to be in jail more than that guy. The Prohibition law's made criminals out of enough hard working men who're trying to put food on the table."

Grayson Dunlop appeared at that moment. He sat down warily.

"Hello, Grayson," said Vickers.

"Nice to see you again," said Max.

"I'll get right to the point," said Vickers. "We arrested one of your bootlegger friends this morning. We know you're pals with him, but we'd like to hear your side of the story first."

"S..story? What do you mean?" Dunlop stalled for time to think.

"We can hold you for questioning without a charge for 24 hours and that's just what we're going to do if you get amnesia all of a sudden. You'd better come clean and you'd better do it now."

Dunlop folded his arms. "I got nothing to say."

"No? You don't want to tell us about how you're a middleman for a rum running syndicate? That's a shame. It's a good story. Of course, you don't have to cooperate. I'm sure the judge would understand."

"J...judge?"

"Of course, we got us a witness that can testify to your little part time job, so I guess we can do without you telling us about it, but we sure would appreciate it."

Dunlop looked skeptical, but finally put his head in his hands. "All right. It's true. I ran into a friend about a year ago and he asked if I would help him out on a part time basis with a little business venture he was in. I didn't realize what I got myself in for at first, but it seemed harmless enough. I've been acting as a go-between for over a year, but I don't really do that much. I just make contacts and handle payments sometimes, maybe once a month. There's not much to it. Some guy provides liquor to the syndicate for shipment and the syndicate gives me the money to pay him. Or maybe the syndicate provides a shipment locally, and the speakeasy pays me and I pay the syndicate. That way, they only deal with one outsider instead of dozens. There's less chance of anyone blabbing to the law that way."

Max decided to take a stab in the dark. "And that money you lost with Leroux was syndicate money, wasn't it?"

There was a long pause. Finally, Dunlop said "Yes. All of it. Sometimes I'd get the money from the speakeasies a week before I had to pay it to the syndicate. I figured I could use it to make a quick profit on a hot stock. It worked once or twice, but then I had a bad streak."

Max and Vickers looked at each other.

"And do the people in the syndicate know what happened to their money?" Max asked.

"I don't think so. I've been stalling them, but they're getting insistent. I'm getting a bank loan tomorrow to pay them, now that I have no chance to get it from Leroux."

"Did Leroux know about what you've been doing with the syndicate?"

"No. I never told anyone. I wanted to. I wanted to ask him to loan me the money, but I didn't."

"Were you afraid?" asked Max.

"Afraid and ashamed. I decided to pay back the money, then get out altogether. It isn't worth it."

"I suppose you realize how this looks in view of the murder," said Vickers.

"In view of the murder? What do you mean?"

Max took up the questioning. "I think what the chief is driving at is the fact that this opens up several new possibilities. Possibility number one is that you might have killed Leroux to get the money you needed."

"What? No! Besides, I read that the police found his money was still there."

"That's true," said Max, "but since we have no idea how much money he had *before* he was murdered, it raises the possibility that you stole just enough to pay your debt and left the rest to make it look like it wasn't a robbery."

"But...but..."

"The second possibility," Max continued, "is that the syndicate boys might have killed Leroux for the money themselves, or perhaps they thought you had told him about your arrangement and they were afraid he would talk."

Dunlop looked as if he was about to faint. "No. No. I never told them anything. Never."

"All right, Mr. Dunlop," said Vickers. "You are free to go for now. We may be seeing you again when we gather a bit more evidence. We will need the names of the syndicate people before this is over. Meanwhile, don't leave town."

Dunlop got to his feet like a man in a daze. "All right..."

"Oh, and pay back your friends before they do something rash, would you?"

When Dunlop was gone, Max looked out the window.

"So now we have bootleggers and embezzlement to add to the mix. One thing this case didn't need was more complication."

*John Reisinger*

## Chapter 15
### Bootleggers and an angel


After dinner that evening, (Frankfurters and beans cooked in a big pot and only slightly burned) Allison sat in a front porch wicker chair in front of her typewriter going over her notes on the proposed bay bridge. Max came out on the porch and kissed her on the forehead.

"How's the article coming?"

"Well, I have most of the information I need, but one thing I learned at the Sunpapers is the need to cover both sides of the story."

"Meaning?"

"Meaning I really should talk to some people in Philadelphia about their view of the bridge project."

"I can save you the trouble," said Max; "they're against it."

"I realize that, but I really should cover their point of view."

Max sat in the wicker chair next to her. "I suppose that would give the article a certain balance. The problem will be finding a time to abandon your press briefing duties."

"I think I can skip a day. That's all it will take. I'm thinking of leaving right after the morning briefing tomorrow. I can take the train from Easton to Clayton in Delaware and then straight up to Philadelphia. I can be back the next afternoon."

"Fine by me, but it might put the mayor in a panic."

"He'll survive. I really need to do this."

"It sounds like a good idea. I believe there's a train from Easton in the early afternoon. You can be there in less than three hours."

"Which brings up another item."

'Yes?"

"I sent a special delivery letter to Mrs. Leroux yesterday."

"You what? Why would you do that?"

"I knew I'd need to go up to Philadelphia and I wanted to see if I could have a chat with her while I was there."

"But she's already refused to talk," Max objected.

"She's refused to talk to the police. Maybe she'd talk with another woman, one who isn't in law enforcement."

"Well...maybe. I suppose it's worth a try, but why didn't you tell me?"

"I wanted to truthfully say that you didn't know I was contacting her. I thought it would make my overture less threatening that way."

Max nodded. "Good strategy. What did you say?"

"I appealed to her to help you find her husband's killer. I assured her you were not with the police and that I would not try to use whatever information she gave me against her, only against the killer. I also assured her we were not trying to pin the crime on her. Of course, if the facts point that way, it may happen anyway."

"Hmmm," said Max.. "I've learned never to underestimate your powers of persuasion, so it just might work. Anything I can do?"

She got up and sat in Max's lap. "Just keep on finding a pregnant woman endlessly fascinating."

Max embraced her. "No problem there."

"So what are your plans?"

"Well, I thought after I finished my coffee, I'd whisk you upstairs to bed, my love."

"I meant tomorrow," she said, nuzzling his ear.

"Oh, that. Well, I have to meet a client, up near Denton first thing in the morning, then I'm meeting Glenn and Jacqueline Stilwell at his office in the Stilwell Building to see if I can make any sense out of this crazy search for a nonexistent painting."

"Are you still worrying about that dumb art book?"

"Allison, you know me. I can't stand loose ends or things that don't make sense. This painting thing is both. Anyway. I convinced the chief I should question them alone to keep the volatile Mr. Stilwell from getting defensive at police questioning."

"Good idea," said Allison. "Now if you can just keep him from getting defensive at Max Hurlock questioning..."


Glenn Stilwell was already pacing the floor of his office when Max arrived from his Denton meeting with the art book under his arm the next morning. Jacqueline Stilwell stood looking out the window, and Ned Gunther sat glowering in a corner. To Max, it looked like an assembly of the bereaved, only grumpier.

Max looked around the room. It was roomy, but plainly furnished, with one barred window, two desks, some tables and chairs, and a walk in safe with the door open. On one wall was a Chesapeake Bay navigation chart, and a framed photo of the Stilwell yacht. On another was an architect's drawing of the floor plans of the building, showing the various tenant spaces.

"All right Max," said Glenn Stilwell, firing the opening salvo, "you got us all here. Are you prepared to arrest someone yet? Look at this headline in the Baltimore Sun. This case is becoming a circus!"

## BOOTLEGGERS CONNECTED WITH
## BUCKET SHOP MURDER

*Police uncover syndicate connection at Stilwell Building*

*Mysterious Violet found; what is her connection?*

"And why are the police questioning our maid? Do they think she took time off from her dusting to commit a locked room murder?" Gunther asked.

Max shook his head. "Look. I admit the loose ends are still flapping in the breeze, but I have to ask you to help clear up a few of them."

"For heaven's sakes," said Jacqueline, "what could *we* clear up? The case looks like it's taking on a life of its own."

"I understand this is where you meet tenants and keep track of the building, Mr. Stilwell."

"Yes. It's sort of my informal office when I'm in town as well. But you already knew that, didn't you?"

"Well, yes," Max admitted. "That's really not why I asked to speak to you. There's been another interesting development."

"And can we expect one of these 'interesting developments' to actually lead to an arrest one day?" Jacqueline Stilwell said, with ice in her voice.

"I think that's very likely, but there's a bit more digging to do first. You see, we have information that Mr. Leroux was making inquiries about a painting."

"Did you say a painting?" said Jacqueline. She pronounced the word "painting" as if it were a disease.

"That's right," said Max. "This painting." He opened the book to the Smiling Angel of Reims. The Stilwells and Ned Gunther craned their necks for a closer look. Max watched their reactions closely. Jacqueline and Gunther looked blankly, but Max thought Glenn seemed startled momentarily...or maybe it was his imagination.

"Very pretty," said Glenn Stilwell, "but what does it have to do with us?"

"Mr. Leroux seemed to think the painting might be in your possession."

"This painting?" said Jacqueline, her mouth opening in amazement. "Where on earth did he get that idea?"

165

"We don't know why he thought so, but he seemed to think it might even be at Casa Leone."

Before either of the Stilwells could reply, Ned Gunther spoke up. "I can answer that, Mr. Hurlock. I keep an inventory of everything in the house and I could recite a description of painting or decoration hanging on those walls. There is absolutely nothing like that; never has been."

"He's right," said Jacqueline, examining the picture closely. "Why, it says here this thing is by Titian, for heaven's sakes. Titian! I wouldn't be able to sleep at night if we had anything like that under our roof. Max, you've been to Casa Leone. You know we have very few pictures to go with the tapestries. We are not art collectors. Our paintings are mostly landscapes selected because the colors go with the décor. I doubt we paid over $200 for anything in the house. The idea we would have anything like this is absurd. If Mr. Leroux thought we did, he clearly had us mixed up with someone else. Either that or he was delusional."

"And he never asked you about a painting. Or maybe hinted about it?" Max asked.

Glenn shook his head. "Not a damned word."

Max rose to leave. "Well, that's what I wanted to clear up. Thanks for your time. He stopped at the floor plans on the wall and pointed at a section.

"This is Leroux's space here?"

Glenn Stilwell nodded. "Yes, right next to mine. Then next to him is Marsha Tolley's real estate office, and so on. As you can see, we're fully leased. Well, we were."

Max squinted and put his finger on another part of the floor plan. "And what is this small room..."

"That's not a room. That's the chase where the chimneys from the fireplaces came up when the place was a hotel years ago, before central heating was installed. I thought it was a waste of space, so I put that walk-in safe there when I renovated the place. It's still a waste of space. I hardly use the safe. It's sort of a giant file cabinet."

"What do you keep in the safe?"

Stilwell made a sweeping gesture with his hand. "Look for yourself. The door is always open when I'm in the office. It saves a lot of dial twisting if I want to get papers."

Max glanced in and saw several shelves with ledgers and papers. On one shelf was a few large envelopes, and a cigar box with a few dollars in it. Otherwise, the safe was empty.

"Say," said Max. "Could the killer have pulled off the locked room trick by using this old chimney chase somehow?"

Glenn shook his head. "Impossible. The thing's been bricked up at every level for years. I had to clear away rubble just to put the safe in. Besides, as I'm sure you saw, there is no opening into Leroux's space."

"I came to the same conclusion," said Max. "Well, another lead falls apart. This is getting to be a habit."

At the press briefing that day, Allison acknowledged that Grayson Dunlop's name had been found in a notebook taken from a suspected bootlegger, but emphasized that the bootlegging charges were unclear at this time, so no real conclusions could be drawn. It wasn't unusual, Allison pointed out, for people on the Eastern Shore to have a wide circle of apparently unrelated acquaintances. Allison thought it best not to tell about the painting, since it would bring unwanted attention to the Stilwells and because it wasn't leading anywhere anyway. Bob Avery, showing off his status as a reporter, asked some thoughtful questions; Chip Carswell was disappointed his scoop didn't seem to be as big as he had thought, and Al White tried, without success, to obtain the name and address of all the witnesses.

"I know the guy they arrested for bootlegging," Chip told Allison at one point. "He's been making his own whiskey for years. He's pretty small time, but there's no doubt he's a bootlegger. Are you saying he won't be prosecuted?"

"Probably not."

"Geez, what does it take to convict someone of bootlegging around here?"

"The same thing it always takes, Chip; evidence. And unless he is convicted, it's hardly fair to accuse Grayson Dunlop of a crime simply because his name appeared in a phone book. The Easton Police have a good record of arresting and convicting bootleggers, but sometimes the case falls short."

"Forget that!" Al White interrupted. "It's the murder we're interested in. How close are we to an arrest?"

"We're a day closer than we were yesterday. Otherwise, I can't say because I don't know."

Bob Avery spoke up. "I heard there is some sort of rare painting involved. Could you comment?"

Allison was taken aback briefly, but recovered. "I think involved is too strong a word, Bob. A book about Renaissance paintings was found in Mr. Leroux's office and Mr. Hurlock has made some inquiries to see if it means anything, but it seems to be unrelated to the crime."

After the briefing, Allison talked to Bob. "Well, Bob, you've come a very long way from the woman-chasing junior reporter who wrote tiny articles about obscure baseball teams."

Bob grinned. "I owe it all to you, Allison. You kept telling me to buckle down and leave the women alone. Finally, I realized you were right and things sort of took off from there."

"So, as my reward you come here to bedevil me. Is that it?"

"Aw, gee Allison. You mean the art book thing? That was nothing. I was hanging around here yesterday and saw them putting it back in the evidence box for the case. One of the cops said Max had borrowed it again, so I figured he'd been asking about it. That made me wonder what he found out."

Allison nodded. "Impressive. A true reporter gambit. Congratulations, Bob."

Bob smiled. "All in a day's work for Bob on the Job.

As soon as Bob left, Allison picked up a small suitcase she had packed and walked to the Easton station to catch the train to Philadelphia. As the train pulled out, she went over her notes and several pages of information about bridge design and construction Max had provided. A little over three hours later, she was standing in front of the Locust Street offices of the Philadelphia Merchants and Steamship Association. Inside, Mr. Taylor Bottomly, Esq ushered her into his office.

"I read a wide range of articles in popular magazines, Mrs. Hurlock," he said, once she was seated and had been offered coffee, "and I have seen some of your work. That's why I was glad to oblige when you asked to talk about the proposed bridge across the Chesapeake."

"Thank you, Mr. Bottomly. I understand that your association is opposed to the bridge, but I try to cover all points of view in an article such as this."

"Yes. Yes; of course. Sound thinking. Well, we are, as you say, opposed to the bridge. Some of our objection, admittedly, is self-interest. It would be foolish to deny it to an intelligent woman such as yourself. The bridge would siphon off to Baltimore some of the shipping that is currently going to Philadelphia. Naturally, we don't want that to happen."

"Well, your honesty is refreshing," said Allison. "I expected a spirited list of the bridge's dangers."

Bottomly smiled. "Oh, I'm coming to that. Just as a defense attorney's job is to find objections to the idea that his client might be guilty, I believe there are some serious problems with the proposed bridge."

"I'm all ears, Mr. Bottomly."

"Now, putting aside the tremendous engineering and financial problems the bridge will involve, and they are many, we believe the bridge would be a threat to both boat traffic, and the economic health of the region."

"Really? That sounds pretty serious."

"The bridge is proposed to connect the Middle River area near Baltimore with the Tolchester-Rock Hall area on the Eastern Shore as you know. If a section of the bridge were to collapse, it could block the main shipping channel and the Intercostal Waterway in that area. I have statistics on the amount of trade that uses the upper bay through the Chesapeake and Delaware Canal to the Delaware River and I don't think you folks in Maryland would want to lose it any more than we would."

"But is a bridge collapse really realistic?"

"If you recall, a German submarine, the *Deutschland*, went all the way up the bay to Baltimore in 1916. We weren't in the war yet, so the crew members were treated as celebrities, but what would prevent such a vessel from attacking the bridge in time of war?"

"Well, I suppose..."

"And," said Bottomly, warming to his theme, "what about hurricanes? One hurricane heading up the bay could leave the bridge wrecked and cutting off the entire area."

"But there are thousands of bridges all over the world and very few collapse," Allison reminded him.

"I am not aware of any that present the combination of being in a critical area of a commercial waterway, being in a tidal area that is also subject to flooding from a river such as the Susquehanna, being in the path of hurricanes every year, presenting a prime target in time of war, and requiring new and unproved engineering technologies to build."

Allison wrote notes furiously. "You make your case well, Mr. Bottomly."

"Thank you, Mrs. Hurlock. I would ask you to be open minded in your article. Remember, even affected parties have valid concerns."

Allison finished the interview about four thirty in the afternoon and walked to Dante and Luigi's Restaurant to have a coffee and go over her notes. She went to the phone and called Mrs. Leroux. There was no answer. Should she try showing up there anyway? Should she take a chance and maybe come up empty? While she was pondering this question, a man came up to her table.

"Excuse me miss. Are you waiting for someone?"

Allison sized him up. He was about her age and well dressed. He looked harmless enough, but was obviously working his way up to a pass.

"No," she said simply.

"May I buy you another coffee? They have the best coffee here."

Allison smiled graciously, and stifled the urge to thank him for making a pregnant woman feel attractive. "Thank you anyway. I have to be leaving in a minute."

The man's face fell. "Ah, well. Maybe some other time. I hope you weren't offended."

"Not at all."

"I mean...well...nothing ventured, nothing gained. Sometimes you only get one chance before an opportunity walks out of your life forever. It doesn't hurt to ask. You never know."

"Yes, that's very true. Thank you. You just helped me make up my mind about something."

She went out, hailed a cab and told the driver to take her to the Mrs. Leroux's address on Rittner Street.

*John Reisinger*

## Chapter 16
## Mrs. Leroux

While Allison was on her way to see Marie Leroux in Philadelphia, Max was back at police headquarters after an uneventful day.

"How's it going, Max?" Vickers asked.

"I was hoping you'd tell me. I don't seem to be able to put all these pieces together. The Stilwells insist they don't have that painting and never even heard of it, which is no big surprise because it doesn't exist anymore. Actually, I've been in their house and as a non-expert, I'd say the *Smiling Angel of Reims*, even if it hadn't been destroyed, is so far beyond anything they have there, it would be like finding a luxury ocean liner tied up at a waterman's house. The Stilwells may be many things, but art connoisseur is not one of them."

Vickers shook his head. "Shoot. Max, I told you that was a wild goose chase. Me, I still got my eye on either Grayson Dunlop or maybe Mrs. Leroux."

"What about Marsha Tolley or Harold Santino?"

"Well," Vickers conceded, "I haven't eliminated them, either. Everyone has a motive and no decent alibi. The only ones we can eliminate  so far are Jacqueline Stilwell and the maid, Violet, since they were both at Casa Leone with witnesses the night of the murder. Oh, by the way, we found the name of the syndicate contact in the same notebook that had Grayson Dunlop's name."

"How did you know it was the syndicate guy?" Max asked.

"Detective work! You're not the only gumshoe around here, Max. Every number in that book was local except one. Now watermen generally don't have a whole lot of contacts that involve long distance calls, so it was a simple matter of tracking down his contact. We're going to question him tomorrow."

"Good luck," said Max, "but I think that's a dead end."

Vickers looked hurt. "What do you mean?"

"The rumrunning syndicates make millions and they depend on staying out of sight. If they commit murder, it's over territory or as an enforcement method on someone in their ranks that betrays them. Why risk the publicity of murdering a regular citizen for a few thousand?"

"I don't know," said Vickers, "but we'll see. I got to do something dramatic, Max. The articles in the papers are taking potshots at me and demanding to know when we're making an arrest. Allison's doing a good job keeping them out of my office, but they're getting more critical every day. The mayor keeps calling for updates and I don't know what to tell him."

"Tell him we have several suspects with plausible motives and no alibis. We just have to narrow it down...or maybe find a better one."

"Speaking of which," said Vickers, "we were able to get in touch with the Mayor of Rock Hall yesterday. He confirmed that Will Purdum of the bridge company met with him on the day of the murder and didn't start back to Easton until after six. He couldn't have gotten back before ten and the shots were heard at nine, so that lets him out."

Max nodded. "Good. One fewer to worry about."

Who are you looking at, Max?"

"Nobody's stood out enough for me to feel confident just yet. Violet and Jacqueline Stilwell have good alibis with witnesses. We have Marsha Tolley, who could be a woman scorned, Harold Santino with his deep grudge over losing his money, Grayson Dunlop who needed to get his money back before the syndicate boys got rough, and possibly one of the Stilwells, or their estate manager, Ned Gunther."

Why would the Stilwells want to kill Leroux?" said Vickers.

"I don't know of a specific reason, but there seems to be a lot of friction around the building between Glenn and Jacqueline. We know she didn't do it herself, but she could have arranged it to make Glenn get rid of the place once and for all. Gunther might have done it at the behest of Jacqueline; he seems very loyal to her. Glenn Stilwell doesn't have a motive I'm aware of, but the painting thing still bothers me and it seems to have something to do with him, somehow."

"Like what?" said Vickers.

"At this point, I can't even guess; probably nothing, but I haven't been able to disprove it yet."

"I notice you didn't mention Mrs. Leroux. Have you eliminated her as a suspect?"

"Not at all," said Max, shaking his head. "A spouse is always a suspect, especially when the couple is in the process of getting a divorce. The fact that Leroux moved all the way from Philadelphia to Easton would seem to indicate some deep and serious rift. We just don't know what it is yet. Say, do you have an extra key to Chesapeake Investments?"

"Sure thing, Max. We got an extra key from Glenn Stilwell so we could have access to the crime scene without the original, seeing as how it's evidence and all."

"Could I borrow it? I'd like to stop by the office again."

"You looking for anything in particular? We already went over the place pretty good."

"I'm sure you did," said Max. "But I find that sometimes just sitting and absorbing the atmosphere at a crime scene helps me visualize what might have happened there."

Vickers went to his desk and rummaged in the drawer. "Here you are, Max. Oh; if you solve the case, you will let me know, won't you?"

Max grinned. "You'll be the first."


Mrs. Leroux's house on Rittner Street in Philadelphia was a gracious brownstone town house with gothic-looking gables and stone steps leading up from the sidewalk to a pair of potted palms by the front door. Not knowing what sort of reception she would find, Allison asked the taxi driver to wait while she rang the bell. A small panel in the door slid to one side, like a speakeasy. The screen behind the panel revealed nothing.

"Yes?" came a flat, female voice.

"Mrs. Leroux? I'm Allison Hurlock from Easton, Maryland. I wrote you about finding who killed your husband and how you could help confidentially. Do you have time to talk?"

The door opened, revealing an attractive, middle-aged woman with a steak of gray in her brown hair. Allison also noticed she was wearing black. She looked at Allison suspiciously.

"I'm not with the police, Mrs. Leroux, and neither is my husband." Allison spoke rapidly, in case the door shut again. "Nothing you tell me will be used against you or wind up in the newspapers, but we could really use your help to catch whoever did this."

"The police think I did it and are working to prove it, evidence or not," Mrs. Leroux replied. "My attorney advises me to speak to no one. He says talking will not help me and may hurt me."

"Well, Mrs. Leroux, I never went to law school, but it seems to me that arresting your husband's killer would help you quite a bit. If you can give me some information, it might help make that happen."

Mrs. Leroux seemed to be undecided for a second, then she spoke. "Mrs. Hurlock, you seem sincere, so this is what I will do; I am traveling to Easton in two days to accompany my husband's body back to Philadelphia. I will give you a piece of information now, and if it does not show up in the papers between now and then, I will know you can be trusted, and I will meet with you in Easton at the Hotel Avon and tell you more. Is that acceptable?"

"Of course," said Allison. "Anything you can tell me might help."

"All right. My husband was not in any trouble and did not have any enemies beyond the occasional unhappy customer. He did not go to Easton because he was fleeing from anyone or anything. He did, however, have a very determined admirer; a local woman named Marsha something or other."

"Marsha Tolley?"

"Yes. That's it. Anyway, Charles was something of a flirt, especially when dealing with a woman who could be helpful to him. This Marsha pushed him and he kept putting her off by telling her our divorce wasn't final, which was true enough. The week before he was killed, she threatened to write me a letter telling all. I suppose she thought that would cause a final break and hurry things along. Charles contacted me to warn me I might get this letter, although I never did. That is all I have to say right now."

Allison would not be back at the Easton train station until well after noon the next day, so Max stopped by a café near the Avon Hotel for a quick dinner before heading home. He sat at a table by the window, ordered a crabcake and watched the traffic. A light rain was falling sporadically, which matched his mood.

"Max! What a pleasant surprise!"

Max looked up and saw Nigel Smythe-Cunningham beaming at him.

"I was on my way back to the hotel when I saw you through the window. Where is your lady wife, the fair Allison tonight?"

"Away researching a story."

"Then perhaps you're in need of company. May I sit down?"

"Sure. I can recommend the crabcake platter. The corn bread alone is worth the price."

Nigel sighed heavily. "I wouldn't want to impose. Maybe just a bit of that crab soup. I've developed a bit of a taste for it. Now where is that waiter?"

"Are you appraising those paintings you mentioned?" Max asked, attacking his crabcake once again.

"Precisely. I'm working my way through the paintings in Mr. Perryman's warehouse. Honestly, with that much pigment, one could paint a goodish sized barn."

Max welcomed the diversion. "Anything of interest?"

"If you mean any smiling angels, I fear not; not even any grumpy ones. Mr. Perryman's collection method apparently was to grab everything and hope there was something valuable."

"An uneven collection?"

"My dear fellow, it's like threshing wheat to extract the grains from the chaff. Several are clearly copies; well, clearly to me. I'm not sure Mr. Perryman realized it. Fortunately, I have no information on how much he paid for any of these works. It might make me weep. Still, there are some valuable pieces among the mediocrities."

"What makes them valuable?" Max asked.

"What makes them valuable is how much someone is willing to pay, and how much one is willing to pay depends on age, the reputation of the artist, and the quality of the work."

Max nodded. "So quality is only one factor?"

"Yes, and not always the greatest, I'm afraid. The artist counts for far more. I could sell a grocery list if Monet or El Greco did it. Of course, one has to be alert for modern day copies. I carry a magnifying glass and a jeweler's loupe to examine signatures or brush strokes, and forceps to pull back the edges of labels or look behind folds in the canvas where it is framed. I suppose evaluating paintings is a form of art itself."

The waiter appeared and Smythe-Cunningham ordered a coffee. "So, how is your murder mystery coming along? No more art related loose ends, I trust?"

"No, I'm afraid not," said Max. "That went nowhere, but it still bothers me. It doesn't fit in."

Smythe-Cunningham nodded sympathetically. "I can sympathize, my dear fellow. I sometimes get obsessed with a painting or some loose bit of information I want to fit into a place it jolly well refuses to go. Look, I don't want to give you the pip by nosing around in your business, but it occurs to me that your art book is like the Egyptian relics in *Death in a Tomb* by Jason Murdock."

"Another mystery?"

"Precisely. A chap is murdered in a museum displaying Egyptian relics. The relics have been rearranged in peculiar patterns and the detective has a deuce of a time trying to figure out what it all means. As it turns out, the killer rearranged the relics to confuse and confound. They meant nothing more."

"And the moral to the story is what?" said Max.

"Well, perhaps the art book and all the curiosity about the *Smiling Angel of Reims* really has no significance beyond the obvious; Charles Leroux wanted to impress women with his sophistication. After all, he never inquired about any painting with Mr. Kirby of the Kirby Gallery in town. It seems to me that anyone actually trying to track down a certain painting would have done that first."

Max looked up sharply from his crabcake. "How do you know he never talked to the Kirby Gallery?"

"I asked Mr. Kirby today. I'm sorry, Max. I hope you don't mind. When I walked past his gallery, I couldn't resist. Call it my little contribution to the case."

Max nodded. "Nigel, that was a true detective move. I'm afraid I never thought of it. Thank you."

Smythe-Cunningham's face lit up. "Think nothing of it old chap. It appears I got to help out in a real murder case after all!"


Allison called from the hotel in Philadelphia that night and told Max of her short talk with Marie Leroux and the need to keep it out of the papers for now.

"Maybe I'll drop by Marsha Tolley's office for a chat," said Max. "I'll tell the chief first, but I have to be careful no one is around to overhear."

"Some way to run an investigation, huh?" said Allison.

"Play the hand you're dealt, I guess. Sleep tight. I'll see you tomorrow when you get back."

After they said goodbye and hung up the phones, Allison sat on the end of the bed looking out the window at the lights of the Philadelphia skyline. She missed Max and home, and started thinking about the baby once more. She was excited for the new addition, but worried about the terrible stories some women had told her about childbirth, childhood diseases, and the chaos brought on by a child in the house. She was trying to think of something else when the phone rang. She grabbed it excitedly.

"Max?"

"Sorry, dear. It's just me."

"Mother! Hello. How did you know I was here?"

"I just called the house and Max gave me the number at the hotel. He told me how busy you'd been for the past few days, and I thought it would be a good time to say hello."

"Never better. I'm just sitting here counting the hours until I can go back home."

"Allison, you should enjoy the chance to travel. Once the baby comes, it will be a bit harder."

"Et tu, Mother?" she mumbled, louder than she meant to. If her Mother heard, she gave no indication.

"Yes," Allison said. "My friends have been telling me all about the horrors of childbirth, the ravages of measles and mumps and the terrors of home life with a child."

Her mother laughed. "Well, there's some truth in all of that, I suppose. Childbirth can have complications and being a parent means doing a lot of things you don't want to do and not doing things you do want to do. It can be tiring, worrying, exasperating, and downright maddening."

Now even my mother is piling on, Allison thought.

"...but Allison, here's something I'll bet your well-meaning friends might have left out; it's all worth it. All the sleepless nights and all the weariness, and all the frustration and all the worry are nothing compared to the joy of bringing a life into this world, nurturing it and making it strong. Allison you are going to have an experience that will be the most rewarding of your life. You are going to create an extension of you and Max; a living person. Nothing you ever do again will compare. Yes, you will have problems and pain, but you will experience moments that will nourish your soul for the rest of your days. From the first moment you hold that tiny hand in yours you will realize that you'll be holding that hand one way or another the rest of your time on this earth. And when you're gone, you will live in your children, and even in their children. It's the closest thing to immortality you will get in this life."

"Whew. Talk about holding hands...You certainly know how to say the right thing when it's needed most," Allison said.

"Of course, dear. I'm a mother."


Not wanting to try his hand at cooking, Max stopped by Bemis's General Store and picked up one of Betty Bemis's famous (in St Michaels) sandwiches for breakfast the next day. As he was getting in his car, he spotted a

Reo truck with *Cassidy Plumbing* on the side, and next to it was Max's friend from high school, Pat Cassidy himself.

"Hey, Pat. How are you?"

"Hey, Max; still solving murders?"

"Sometimes."

"I'll bet you have your hands full with that bucket shop thing in Easton."

"How did you know I'm involved in that?"

"Shoot, Max. Not many secrets around here."

"Say, Pat. I heard you were out at Harold Santino's place the other night."

"Yeah. He needs a new well pump, but he's been putting it off."

"And Harold says you were there around seven thirty?"

Cassidy frowned. "Seven thirty? Naah. Old Harold's confused. I was supposed to be there at seven thirty, but got held up on another job and didn't get there until after nine. I guess he needs to get his clock fixed, too."

"Are you sure about that time, Pat?"

"Of course; time is money."

Max thanked him and went home. So it seemed that Harold Santino had a perfectly good alibi and didn't even realize it. Well, scratch him off the suspect list.

The next morning, Max took Vickers aside and told him about Harold Santino's newfound alibi and what Allison had found out.

"This has to be kept quiet until Marie Leroux comes here in two days to claim the body, but maybe I can have an informal chat with Marsha Tolley in the meantime."

"Just so no one overhears, Max. If word gets into the press it could make Marie Leroux clam up for good."

Marsha Tolley was pleased to see Max again, and offered him a hot cup of tea. Max declined.

"So tell me Max, are you getting close to an arrest?"

"Closer than last time we talked, but we're not there yet. I'm just following up on our last conversation."

She nodded and took a sip of her tea. "I appreciate that nothing I told you before wound up in the Star-Democrat. My relationship with Mr. Leroux was...private."

"Yes, well, that's what I wanted to ask you. I understand his upcoming divorce was not proceeding very quickly."

Marsha Tolley took a sip of tea and daubed her lips with a napkin. "Not at all. At first I blamed his wife, but later, it appeared to me that Charles was really not forcing the issue the way he should have."

"Is that why you threatened to write a letter to his wife a week before he died?"

"Who told you that?" She looked startled.

"It doesn't matter who told me. Is it true?"

Marsha Tolley sat silently a moment.

"Anything you say will not be in the papers. You have my word."

"All right," she sighed. "I did threaten to write to his wife, but I wasn't really going to do it, Max."

"No?"

"Of course not. It was just a foolish ploy to knock him out of his complacency. I thought it might lend some urgency to whatever efforts he was making. I'm a little ashamed now."

Max remained silent, encouraging her to say more.

"Max, I'm 33 years old. My first husband died in the war. I don't know how often someone like Charles will come along. He was kind and witty, and well read. Did you know he was a Captain in the French army in the war? He's been all over France and a lot of Germany before he came here. The stories he would tell! Well, I was infatuated with him and I saw him slipping away. I guess it was stupid."

"Not to mention making you look guilty. A woman scorned and all that..."

"I know, but there is nothing I can do about it now. At least I never wrote any letter."

"Then you weren't angry with him?"

"Of course I was. I get angry with some of my clients, too, but I don't murder them! Look, Charles's death is a scar on my heart. There is no way I would have wanted anything to happen to him. Why did you think I'm talking to you? On the chance that some small thing I remember might help find the killer. Believe me, no one will be happier to see justice done than I will!"

Afterwards, Max was out on the sidewalk in front of the Stilwell Building when he suddenly remembered the key the chief had loaned him. The rain was starting to drizzle and he didn't look forward to a wet walk back to the police station, so he went back inside and let himself into the now empty office of Chesapeake Investments. He shut the door behind him and looked over the room. The stillness was broken only by the soft drip of raindrops on the windowpane. Outside, a car passed by with a hissing of tires on wet pavement. Max walked over to the desk, his heels making hollow noises on the wooden floor, and sat in Leroux's swivel chair. Through the transom, he could hear the sound of someone walking down the stairs and going out the front door. Then all was silent once again. Max looked around the room, trying to picture the crime. Leroux is at his desk; there is a knock on the door; someone enters; Shots are fired and Leroux falls. But why? And then what?

He looked through the desk drawers, now empty. He walked around to the back room. The bathroom, the closet, and even the section of brickwork being repaired under the window, but nothing gave up its secrets. He went back to the chair and looked around. Directly across from him was the big chalkboard with the stock names and prices. He looked at the board, the chalk tray, the eraser, and even the bits of chalk dust here and there. He went over the stocks listed one by one for anything wrong or unusual, but there was nothing.

It wasn't working. The room held its secrets as tightly as before. Finally, he rose and started for the door with one last glance at the chalkboard. There, on the floor below where it met the wall, was a very slight sprinkle of chalk dust. He remembered seeing that sort of thing in school. He tried to ignore it, but his sense of order wouldn't let him. He had to clean it up. Finally, he bent over and wiped up the dust with his handkerchief. He noticed it made a scratching noise when he drew he cloth over it.

"Gritty chalk dust?" he said aloud. He rolled some dust between his fingers, feeling the rough texture, then he picked up some chalk dust from the chalk tray. It was smooth. Whatever the dust on the floor might be, it clearly wasn't chalk dust.

"The dust on the floor seems to have come from behind the chalkboard," he mumbled. He looked from below and saw nothing. The board was tight against the brick wall. He looked on the left side of the frame and felt with his fingers a thin piece of rounded metal between the frame and the wall.

A hinge.

He pulled on the chalkboard but it remained solidly in place. He looked on the right side of the frame and found no hinge. He looked closer.

A latch.

He twisted it open and pulled on the chalkboard. The board swung away from the wall. For a moment, Max stood staring, then he stepped to the desk, picked up the phone, and called Chief Vickers.

"Tom? This is Max. I'm over at Chesapeake Investments. You'd better get over here now."

## Chapter 17
## The wall

Allison looked out of the window of the Pullman car at the soft gray rain and listened to the clicking of the tracks. The gentle motion of the train as the car rocked back and forth was soothing, and she sat contentedly daydreaming of impending motherhood. She smiled when she thought of her good-natured banter with Max about whether the baby would be a boy or girl, when they both knew it really didn't matter. Their baby would get lots of love and attention whatever it was. Raindrops slowly zig zagged their way down the window of the Pullman car as Allison settled comfortably in the soft cushions. It was nice to put the murder out of her mind for a while. As the train crossed into Delaware, she wondered what Max was doing.

"I hope he can find something to break open this case. It seems like he's hit a brick wall."

Allison didn't know how true that was.

Max and the chief stood staring in disbelief at the chalkboard swung out from the wall. Behind was the brick wall, but in the section covered by the chalkboard, someone had removed dozens of the bricks, revealing the second layer behind it. That layer was chipped, but was still intact.

"I think this explains why Leroux worked so many late nights," said Max. "After hours, no one would hear him hammering or chipping. Plus, no one would see him hauling away the debris when he left."

"What do you suppose he was up to, Max?"

"It looks like he was trying to get to whatever was on the other side of this wall, and I think I know what it is."

"Well, don't keep me in suspense."

"Glenn Stilwell's office is on the other side of this wall. I paced it off and it looks like that hole will be in the area of Glenn Stilwell's walk-in safe."

"He was trying to get in the safe? Through the wall?"

"It's actually pretty clever," said Max. "The door of a walk-in safe is the strongest part, but because the interior of the safe is usually surrounded by concrete, or in this case masonry, the side walls are usually just thin sheet metal. It would be a lot easier getting in this way, and it can be done without the safe owner's knowledge."

"So what do you suppose is in that safe that's worth all this?"

Max frowned and scratched his head. "That's the problem; I have no idea. I've had a quick look at the inside of the safe when I was in that office and it's almost empty. Unless Glenn Stilwell had some microfilm or gems stashed where I couldn't see them, this whole effort on the part of Leroux doesn't make sense."

"Maybe Stilwell had something in the safe at the time, but he moved it."

"Yeah, maybe," said Max. "Well, I guess we'll just have to ask him. But let's not tell him about the wall just yet."

"Don't tell him about the wall? Why not?"

"I don't know," said Max, "but somehow I think it might be to our advantage to keep that quiet for a while."

Glenn Stilwell wasn't happy about the prospect of driving to his Easton office on a rainy day, but showed up a half hour later.

"All right, Max. You and the chief here seem to think you found something important I should see. Let's get on with it."

Since Stilwell was no fan of the chief, Max took the lead.

"As I said on the phone, there's been an important development. We have received information that Charles Leroux was very interested in the contents of your safe."

Stilwell looked confused. "My safe? Why would he be interested in my safe? It's hardly the bank."

"That's what we're trying to find out. Would you open the safe, please?"

Stilwell complied, and with a few twists of the dial, the door swung open. Max and Vickers looked inside carefully. The safe was about five feet square inside with shelves on each sidewall and a narrow isle in the center. Max stepped into the safe and looked around. The shelves looked as bare as Max remembered.

"You don't keep anything valuable in this safe?"

"Just some papers, a few office supplies and maybe $200 in petty cash."

"What's this in the back?" asked Max. He reached in and pulled out a large mailing envelope then pulled out what was inside. "Well, well; a .32 caliber pistol."

Stilwell shrugged. "Just a little insurance policy in case anyone shows up trying to rob me. I figure I just go in the safe for the money, then give a bandit a little lead surprise."

Max sniffed the barrel. "It's been fired recently."

Stilwell was calm. "Of course. I take it back to Casa Leone once in a while to fire it to make sure it's in working order. I did that about a week ago."

"I'm afraid we'll have to borrow this for a while, Mr. Stilwell," said Max.

"Wait a minute. Are you saying you think *I* had something to do with the murder?"

"We have to check every lead, Mr. Stilwell," said Vickers. "You have to admit that a man is possibly killed by *your* gun while inquiring about *your* safe does raise a few questions."

"I don't give a damn what it raises. You tried to frame my wife for murder, and now you're trying to frame me!"

"It's all right, Glenn," said Max in what Allison always called his "reasonable" voice. "The police have to follow up on things like this. They would be remiss if they didn't. Meanwhile, it would be helpful if you could try to remember any conversation you had with Leroux that would have led him to think you had something valuable in that safe."

"Look, you two..." Stilwell had calmed down, but was still far from tranquil. "I do not have anything valuable in that safe, I have never had anything valuable in that safe, I have never told Leroux or anyone else I had anything valuable in that safe, and I never even *hinted* I ever had anything valuable in that safe."

"And I believe you said that on the night of the murder, you were on your boat alone?"

"That's right. Now if you will excuse me, I have other things to do."

Max and Vickers stood outside on the sidewalk discussing what to do next.

"I'm going to get this gun over to the sergeant to see if he can find any way of matching it to the murder weapon. All I know is that it's the same caliber and was fired recently."

Max nodded absently. "Uh huh. Well, I'm going back in and check with the other tenants to see if the safe door was open any time they were in Stilwell's office."

A few minutes later, Max emerged once more, from the Stilwell Building. He had found seven tenants; two had been in Stilwell's office at various times in the last few months. All of them remembered the safe door being wide open and four of them had gotten a good look inside. They all described the safe as being almost empty and certainly containing nothing that looked in any way valuable. As one of them pointed out, why would he leave the door open if he kept anything valuable in there? It was a good question, and one Max couldn't answer.

That afternoon, Max met Allison at the Easton station on Pennsylvania Avenue. The rain had stopped and Allison alighted from the train with enthusiasm. Like actors in a romantic film, they ran to each other and embraced.

"Max! I had a wonderful trip, but I missed you."

"Same here. The place was empty without you, but it sounds as if your sojourn in Philadelphia was worthwhile. You got good information for your article and got Mrs. Leroux talking, at least a little."

They started walking down the train platform to the waiting car.

"Yes, and I keep thinking about what she said about her husband not having serious enemies and not coming to Easton because he was on the run. But why did he come to Easton in the first place? I mean, if you're living in Philadelphia, you don't just strike your tent, pack up your camels, and head for a small town on the Eastern Shore to start over unless there's some good reason."

"Well," said Max, "I might have stumbled on a partial answer. It seems Charles Leroux was apparently attempting to tunnel through his party wall and into Glenn Stilwell's safe."

Allison stopped on the train platform and dropped her handbag. "Jeepers! That changes things. Tunneling through a brick wall? So what was he trying to get?"

"Well, that's the problem. I don't know. There is nothing of value in that safe, and as far as I've been able to find out, there never has been."

Allison frowned in thought for a moment. "Maybe Leroux somehow thought there was something there, but there wasn't."

"It's possible, but what? Oh, and there's one other thing."

"Still more? My, you have been busy in my absence."

"We did find a recently-fired .32 caliber pistol in Stilwell's safe."

"Yikes! Well that's a big clue. So maybe Glenn Stilwell found out that Leroux was after whatever he had and killed him?"

Max shook his head. "I didn't say that."

"But it's possible, isn't it? I mean, a man like Glenn Stilwell is wealthy enough to have jewels, gold bars, or who-knows-what in that safe."

"In theory, but if he did, nobody seems to have been aware of it but Charles Leroux."

"Yes, that is odd," said Allison, frowning. "The funny thing about this case is that the more you find out, the less you seem to really know."

The press briefing that day was later in the afternoon. Allison reported that the police were investigating several new possibilities, but that she was not able to provide any more information just yet.

"What sort of new information are they investigating?" Al White asked.

"Is this information related to the meeting between the police chief, Max Hurlock, and Glenn Stilwell this morning?" Bob Avery asked.

Where was he getting his information? Allison thought. "The chief and Max are meeting with a variety of different people and following several different leads."

"So what does Max think was in Glenn Stilwell's safe?" Chip Carswell asked.

"What makes you think a safe is involved?" Allison couldn't help asking.

"I talked to some of the tenants at the Stilwell Building before I came here. They told me Max was asking about Glenn Stilwell's safe."

"Come on, Chip. You know Max asks about a lot of things. You do the same thing. You have to do that to get to the bottom of a case like this."

"And has he reached the bottom yet?" said Al White.

"Not yet, but when he does, you'll be the first to know, I promise."

Max came by after the press briefing to pick up Allison and found her slumped on a bench outside police headquarters as he pulled up to the curb. She looked as tired as he'd ever seen her.

"Hello Max."

"Allison; you look exhausted. Come on, let's go home."

"In a minute, Max. I don't know if it's the last two days, or junior making his or her presence known, but I could do with a serious nap right about now."

He sat next to her. "I know. This case has been taking a lot out of both of us. This is one time we can't escape.

Even when we go home, we're still practically in the middle of it. Well, it won't last much longer."

"Neither will I."

"All right, my love. Time for you to return to Chez Hurlock. Up and at 'em."

"Hey, Max!" Chief Vickers was calling from the police headquarters doorway.

"Sorry, Tom. I'm going home, and taking my bride with me."

Vickers caught up with them just as Max was helping Allison into the Model A. "I just wanted to tell you we've been examining that gun we found in Glenn Stilwell's safe and comparing the bullets with the ones that killed Leroux."

"And...?"

"We can't say for sure it's the same gun. The results were inconclusive."

Max nodded. "Just like everything else in this case. Good night, Tom."


After a light dinner of various leftovers from the icebox, Allison went to bed and fell asleep instantly. Max washed up the dishes, then went upstairs to check on her. She was still sleeping soundly. He walked into the baby's room and looked around at the walls that would soon look down on their first child. Then he went into the spare room and looked over their trophies once again. It all seemed so long ago, now, and the old cases seemed so much easier; so much simpler. Now, Allison was exhausted from working on her article while trying to keep the press at bay, and he was treading water on a case where he had no idea why the victim was killed, let alone who did it. Was he losing his touch? Why had he spent so much time chasing around after an art book? The old Max wouldn't have gone off on a tangent like that, would he?

His mind drifted back to the art book again. He couldn't help it. He forced the thought from his mind and went downstairs and read the newspaper.

The headline told of the voyage of the Norge, an airship that had set out to make the first overflight of the North Pole with an Italian, American and Norwegian crew. The Norge had crossed the pole and dropped flags, then lost contact for two days. Now the Norge had been found again. A storm had forced a landing in an Eskimo village. Max couldn't help comparing this adventure with his own plodding efforts to track down the whys and hows of the murder of Charles Leroux.

He wanted to talk it out with Allison, but she needed sleep now more than he needed counsel. He sat on the porch and watched the shadows lengthen. The slow sunset seemed somehow appropriate.

The next morning, Allison was up early, refreshed and ready to meet whatever the day had in store. Max felt better, too, but was still unhappy about how the case was inching from one unsatisfactory revelation to the next, and seemingly getting no closer to a conclusion.

"I feel much better this morning," said Allison. "I really needed that 'sleep that knits up the raveled sleeve of care' that Shakespeare talked about."

"Great. I knew it would take more than a trip to Philadelphia, continuous sparring with the press, and a growing baby to keep you down."

"And how. So what are you planning for today, Max?"

"I thought I'd go through the newspaper files at the Easton library and see if I can dig up anything about Glenn Stilwell that might shed some light. I also thought I'd call an old school friend who works at the National Archives in D.C. They might have some information on Glenn Stilwell's war record that might be pertinent. Tom Vickers has already had someone go to the courthouse to check the general public records and the Clerk of the Court records to see if there are any liens, complaints, lawsuits, or dicey real estate transactions involving the Stilwells or Nick Gunther. He didn't find anything unusual, but maybe I can."

"Hmm. I suppose it's worth a try, but I have a feeling it'll be tough to pin anything on someone that powerful and that secretive."

"Maybe, but I'm starting to think that Glenn Stilwell holds the key to this whole thing. I don't know how just yet, but he's involved, and maybe Jacqueline and Ned Gunther."

"All of them?"

"Who knows?" said Max. "There are wheels within wheels with those three. I'm sure you've noticed that they unite and work together against the outside world, but have their own frictions. Jacqueline and Glenn have knock down-drag out fights occasionally, and Gunther seems to act more as Jacqueline's bodyguard than an estate manager. In a conflict between the Stilwells, Gunther might very well side with Jacqueline. But what it all means, and how it relates to the murder of Charles Leroux, I have no idea at this point."

"Well, I'm sure you'll untangle it, Max. Somehow, you always do."

"Are you coming to Easton with me? I'm stopping by Chesapeake Investments for a while also. This time, I'm bringing a magnifying glass and a folding rule."

"No. I thought I'd stay here and get some work done on my article. Later, I can get a ride up to Easton with Iris Dalrymple in time for the press briefing this afternoon."

"I'm afraid you won't have much to tell at the press briefing."

"That's all right; at the last two, the reporters had more new information than I did. I guess I can't fault them for doing their jobs."

"Maybe not," said Max, "but if they get wind of the gun in the safe, the speculation will be flying so thick you could make soup out of it."

"You're right; there'll be no holding them back. The headlines will almost write themselves. Police now have a motive, a murder weapon, and the Stilwells washing their hands saying 'out damned spot'."

## Chapter 18
## Max keeps digging


The newly opened Easton library was on the second floor of a building just on the other side of the courthouse from the Stilwell Building. It was a clean and bright place with two rooms and several hundred books, but was huge compared to St Michaels, and had a fairly good reference section. Max arrived at the library and placed a long distance call to his friend at the National Archives in Washington. After a few minutes of reminiscing about high school, Max asked if it would be possible to find any public records pertaining to the Stilwells. The friend said it would be simple, and promised to call back with the information that afternoon. Then Max asked the librarian if there was any way of searching old newspapers for articles about specific subjects.

"Sure. The New York Times started publishing a quarterly index of its articles in 1913, and made the books available to libraries as an aid to researchers and as a promotional effort. The articles are indexed by subject and each entry shows a title, location, headline, and sometimes a one sentence summary. Which index would you like?"

Max found an article in 1920 announcing Glenn Stilwell receiving some sort of certificate for his wartime work with the American Embassy in Paris. Another article mentioned Stilwell's name as a participant in a yacht race to Bermuda in 1921, and as the host of a get together for Washington officials at Casa Leone in 1924. Charles Leroux appeared nowhere in the index. The final article mentioned Glenn Stilwell as a member of the board of the Baltimore Steamship and Railroad Trade Association, one of the groups that stood to benefit from a bay bridge if it were ever built. Interesting, Max thought, but hardly the stuff of which murders are made. He looked up Smiling Angel of Reims and found a very short article that had appeared on page 32 that said that a German artillery shell had destroyed the famous painting amidst international condemnation. Unfortunately, there was nothing that Smythe-Cunningham hadn't already told him. Still, he kept digging.

Back in St Michaels, Allison sat on the front porch organizing her notes and working up an outline for her article on the proposed bay bridge. She was toying with a clever opening line that hinted at the various factions involved.

"You can't cross the bay without crossing someone."

Now for a title; well she could work on that later. The trick with an article like this, of course, was to incorporate a lot of facts and statistics in a way that people would still find interesting. Allison planned to work in the facts painlessly among the breezy narrative, and organized the article carefully. She was just about to start typing when the phone jangled inside the house. Thinking it was Max, she rushed in and picked it up.

"Long distance operator," came the scratchy voice over the line. "I have a person to person long distance call from Philadelphia for Allison Hurlock."

"This is Allison Hurlock."

"One moment, please."

Allison sighed, She really didn't need this interruption. I guess Mr. Bottomly thought of some more reasons why a bridge across the bay would spell the doom of civilization, she thought. To her surprise, she heard a woman's voice on the other end.

"Mrs. Hurlock, this is Marie Leroux."

"Hot dog!" whispered Allison.


"Phone call for you, Mr. Hurlock. It's your wife."

At the Easton library, Max looked up from the Times Index and his notes.

"Hey Allison, what's up?"

"The lady I spoke with yesterday just called."

"You mean Mrs..."

"Max, this is a party line; remember?"

"Oh, of course. I know who you mean."

"Well, it seems she talked to her attorney after I left. He's read some of my articles, and said an interview would be a way of getting her side of the story out, sort of a literary self-defense. She's going to arrive in Easton tomorrow and will meet both of us at the Avon at five. She's going to tell all"

"Good going Allison," said Max, "Sometimes I think you could get the Sphinx to talk! ...but did you say 'both of us'?"

"That's right. You're invited, but not the police. She's even using an alias. If the police or reporters appear, she'll clam up."

"This is great news. I haven't found out anything useful yet, but I'm waiting for a call back from my pal at the National Archives. Maybe you should have called him. You seem to have the ability to shake information loose."

"Just natural charm, I guess. See you later."

Max hung up and smiled.

"Say, Max," the librarian interrupted. "Did you see today's Star-Democrat? There's another story about that case you're working on. Here it is."

She held up the paper.

## NEW LEADS IN BUCKET SHOP MURDER

*Police find mysterious Violet who had relationship with victim*

*Could a jilted romance be a motive?*

*"There's always a woman involved," says one Easton man.*

*"I'll bet she was a gold digger," says local woman.*

"Can I see that?" Max asked. "Let's see. Mysterious woman connected to victim...police questioned her, but won't say what she knows...possible connection with unexplained art book...Violet reluctant to come forth...possible jealousy of another woman....I have to admit, Chip Carswell is sticking with it."

He put the paper aside, stood up and stretched.

"I'll be back in an hour or so. If anyone calls, I'll be over at the Stilwell Building."

The Stilwell Building was quiet, and the door to Chesapeake Investments still had a slight creak when Max opened it. The room looked the same. Max went to the chalkboard and swung it out. He looked again at the chipped and ragged brickwork, then took out the magnifying glass he had brought. Inch by inch, Max inspected the bricks. With the magnifying glass, he could see marks left by a chisel, and various scratches and gouges. He stopped. One brick in the center of the inner wall looked different. Unlike the tan, sandy-looking mortar between the bricks everywhere else, the mortar around this brick had a grayish tone...as if fresh.

He picked up the telephone and called police headquarters.

"Tom, this is Max over at Chesapeake Investments. I didn't notice it before, but one of the bricks is newly placed. It looks like someone took it out then put it back, and I don't think it was Leroux. I want to remove the brick and see what's behind it, but I don't want to destroy evidence or search without a search warrant. What are the chances of getting a warrant for Stilwell's office?"

"Out of the question, Max. The judge wouldn't give me a warrant based on what we have. We know Leroux was burrowing through the wall to get to the safe, but we have both seen the safe and examined it. We know there is nothing of value in there, so there is no basis for a warrant. Look; the mayor tells me he's getting calls from various Washington politicians and even the mayor of

Baltimore. The reporters are staying away from our mayor, thanks to Allison, but they're still hot on the scent of a sensational story. We're operating in a fishbowl on this one. We have to be extra careful."

"I understand, Tom. I'll figure out something else," said Max, and hung up.

Max thought a moment, then called Allison at home.

"Allison, what time is your press briefing over?"

"Usually we're done by two. Why?"

"And we're meeting Marie Leroux at the hotel at five?"

"That's right."

"If I can arrange it, could you meet me and the chief at Stilwell's office at two thirty?"

"Sure. What's up?"

"I'll explain everything this afternoon. See you then."

Max put the phone down and noticed the librarian coming toward him.

"Max, have you seen this? It's today's Sunpaper. Just came over on the morning steamboat run from Baltimore to Kent Island."

Max looked at the paper. The Bucket Shop Murder article was series of local comment on the case, a sign of a shortage of real information.

*"The police don't know what they're doing," said local chicken farmer D Smith. "How hard can it be? You find out who had a motive and arrest them."*

*"Mark my words, there's a woman involved," said waterman K. Samuels. "They'll find he was running around and got some woman mad. Happens every time."*

*Meanwhile, Easton shop owner Dee Dee Douglas worries about more murders. "I mean, if a person isn't safe in his own business, where will it all end? I could wind up dead on the floor here, just like poor Mr. Leroux. I'm telling you, they'd better catch this guy fast!"*

"Seem like everybody's got an opinion," said the librarian, "and the less they know, the more sure they are. Well, it's just uninformed speculation."

"Is there any other kind?" Max mumbled.

One of the disadvantages of getting a ride from Iris Dalrymple, Allison thought, is that you become a captive audience for whatever topic Iris wished to expound on that day. Of course, it was usually interesting and educational, but some days you just weren't in the mood.

Today was such a day.

"I read where Hans Luther has just resigned as Chancellor of Germany." She began, "Well, I'm not surprised. The man was supposed to a finance expert and he never did anything about the inflation. Why, things are so bad that workers rush off to spend their wages before they lose their value. People need a wheelbarrow full of Marks to buy a loaf of bread. I'm telling you, some rabble rouser is going to take advantage of that mess and take over the country someday."

"Another Mussolini?" said Allison, trying to be polite.

"Mussolini? Well, let me tell you a thing or two about that bag of wind..."

Finally, Allison made her way to the police headquarters to confront the press once again.

"So I understand your husband admits the case is going slowly and that they don't have enough evidence," Al White started off the proceedings on a sour note.

"Who told you that?" said Allison.

"The librarian. I saw Max going there this morning and asked a few questions when he left."

"My, you do have sources everywhere."

"So how about it?" said Chip Carswell. "Max isn't giving up is he? Is this going to be an unsolved case?"

"Absolutely not. As far as Max is concerned, there are only two kinds of cases; those that are solved and those that are not solved yet."

"A good quote, Allison," said Bob Avery. "I might use it."

"Glad to be of assistance."

"So what were you doing in Philadelphia yesterday?" said Al White.

"Just some research for an article I'm working on...about a bridge over the bay."

"Never happen," said Al White. "There would never be enough demand to make it pay for itself."

"Now I might quote you," said Allison.

"That was off the record."

"Yesterday, a Congressman said the feds should send in the FBI to get this case solved," said Bob Avery. "Would the police welcome their help?"

"Like a picnic welcomes ants," was what Allison wanted to say, but she struggled to keep from making a smart comeback that would wind up in print. "No contact has been made yet, so I don't know under what conditions the FBI would operate. The Easton Police are being assisted by other jurisdictions, including the Philadelphia Police, and are..."

"What are the Philadelphia Police doing," Chip Carswell asked.

"They located Mrs. Leroux up in Philadelphia."

"Any prospects of that dame talking?" said Al White.

"Nothing yet, but we are hoping she'll help out."

"What about that Violet? Is she a suspect?"

Allison sighed.


Max, meanwhile, was back at the library, waiting for the call from the National Archives. To pass the time, he looked through the times index some more, looking up articles about various topics. There really was a wealth of historical information available, he thought. It was almost like having a time machine. Several articles were worth saving.

"Say, could I make a long distance call to New York if I reimburse the library?"

"Sure, just make a note of the time and the number on this slip and sign it afterwards."

Max dialed the long distance operator and asked for the number of the director's office of the Metropolitan Museum of Art in New York. A few seconds later, a secretary answered and said the director was not available.

"Miss, my name is Max Hurlock. I am helping the police investigate a murder case you may have heard of. They're calling it the Bucket Shop Murder. I believe there might be a fine art aspect to this case, and I would like to ask the director some general questions about renaissance paintings. He might just help us solve a murder."

The secretary sounded intrigued. "No kidding?"

"No kidding. I promise not to take up much of his time."

A moment later, a voice came on the phone. "This is Edward Robinson. I understand you wish some information on art for a murder case?"

Max smiled. Everyone wants to get in on a notorious case. "Yes, sir. I've been speaking with Nigel Smythe-Cunningham of the Smythe-Cunningham Gallery in your city, and he's been very helpful, but I'm told that no one knows the art market better than you do. I assume you're acquainted with Mr. Smythe-Cunningham?"

"I am aware of Mr. Smythe-Cunningham and his gallery."

They spoke for about twenty minutes, with Max taking notes furiously. Max thanked him and hung up the phone.

"That'll cost you," said the librarian, shaking his head.

A little while later Max's phone call from his friend at the National Archives came in.

"Hey, Max. This Stilwell guy is the cat's pajamas. He was a Major in the AEF in France during the war, that's the American Expeditionary Force..."

"I know what it stands for," said Max. "I was in the Navy."

"Oh, right. Anyway, he was in the artillery for a while, but I guess he had friends in high places because he got attached to the American Embassy in Paris. Nice duty, even during a war. He was sort of military liaison officially, but what he really was is a spy. He'd make visits to the front and report back on how the French and the Brits were faring. Anyway, he was wounded in 1918 on one of his trips and was sent back to the states and civilian life. He and his wife Jacqueline lived in Pittsburgh and did very well in the steel business before coming to Maryland. That's about all there is. Does that help?"

"Well, it doesn't hurt. Thanks a lot."

After Max hung up, he looked over his notes and made a list.

| *Suspect* | *Possible motive* |
| --- | --- |
| *Glenn Stilwell-* | *Protect his property* |
| *Ned Gunther -* | *Loyalty to Jacqueline* |
| *Marie Leroux-* *reason unclear* | *Angry at husband-* |
| *Grayson Dunlop-* *money* | *Recover bootlegger* |

*Marsha Tolley-*      *Jilted*

*Person unknown-*    *?*


Max pondered the list a long time, then looked at his watch and saw it was almost two thirty. He gathered up his notes and set off for the Stilwell Building.

## Chapter 18
## The secret of the safe

When the briefing was finally over, Allison felt wrung out, but she made her way over to the Stilwell Building to meet Max. When she arrived, she was surprised to see, not only Max, but Chief Vickers standing in the hallway.

"Hello, boys," said Allison. "Come here often?"

"Hey, Allison. How was the press briefing?"

"Briefer than ever. I just have so much new I can tell them. I'm holding back and they know it, but it's all in a day's work. So what are we doing here?"

Max took a deep breath. "Well, I have a plan to find out what Leroux was after, but I don't know if it will work. Either I will be able to finesse a major answer in the case, or my bluff will be called and I'll look like an idiot."

"I see," said Allison, "and this is something you feel is necessary?"

"Without a search warrant, the thing I'm looking for will just stay beyond our reach unless I can pull this off. Ah, here's Mr. Stilwell now."

Glenn Stilwell looked as if he'd rather be somewhere else and he was holding the three of them personally responsible that he wasn't. "All right, Hurlock. I'm here as you asked, but I'm warning you, it had better be worthwhile. I seem to be spending as much time here as at Casa Leone."

"I appreciate it, Mr. Stilwell. I asked Allison to come along because I trust her judgement and her sense of fairness. The chief is here as an official witness."

"Witness to what?"

"Could we all sit down, first?" said Max. They all sat in various chairs around Stilwell's desk and across from the still-locked safe. Max remained standing.

"First of all, Mr. Stilwell, I want to thank you for the level of cooperation you've displayed. In return, Allison here has fenced with the press to try to minimize any bad publicity as we investigated this case."

Stilwell grunted an acknowledgement.

"In that spirit, I've asked you here to cooperate further as a way of saving both time and possible embarrassment. You see, I now know what led up to the murder of Charles Leroux. I don't know all the details, but I do know it revolved around a goal, an object he was seeking. I now know what that object was and I know it is still here. We could ask for a search warrant, but that would become a matter of public record and the town is full of reporters digging around. Therefore, I believe your continued cooperation will make things easier on everyone, especially you."

"Why in the devil would I need things to be easier on me?" Stilwell began to object, but Max ignored him and kept talking.

"For that reason, I am asking you to open the safe."

Stilwell's mouth hung open for a second, and Vickers and Allison looked at each other in astonishment.

"Open the bloody safe? You've already seen it! Hell, you've stepped inside of it. You know every inch of that safe. What do you expect to find that wasn't there before?"

"Please, Mr. Stilwell. I will explain everything in due course. I assure you this is to your advantage."

Stilwell was not convinced. "Look, Max. As far as I know, you're a straight shooter, and Jacqueline thinks highly of Allison here, but the chief has already tried to frame my wife once for a nonexistent crime, so you'll have to excuse me if I get a bit suspicious of oddball requests."

"I swear to you that neither the chief nor even Allison knows about this, as I think you can see by their puzzled expressions."

It was true. The chief looked bewildered and Allison looked as if she wanted to jump in and save Max from the humiliation he seemed to be courting.

The chief shrugged. Allison said "Mr. Stilwell, I don't know what Max has in mind, but I can promise you that he never tries to frame anyone. Never."

"I'm calling my attorney," said Stilwell, reaching for the phone.

"That is certainly your right," said Max, calmly.

Stilwell paused with his hand in midair. "Oh, what the hell. You've already seen it, anyway."

Without another word, Stilwell replaced the phone on its cradle, walked to the safe and opened the door. The inside looked exactly the same as Max remembered it.

"I told you that we found evidence that Charles Leroux was interested in what was in your safe," said Max.

"Yes, you did, and I showed you there was nothing in there to interest anybody," said Stilwell, gesturing towards the open safe door. "There still isn't, and to save you the trouble, there won't be tomorrow, either."

"We also found that Leroux was staying late because he was slowly chipping through the brick wall between your offices opposite where your safe was located."

"What? He was trying to break into my safe?"

"That was how it appeared," said Max, stepping up to the open safe door, "but when I was in the safe the other day, I made a note of its dimensions and I glanced at the floor plan you have on the wall. Today, I was in Leroux's office and was able to measure the exact distance from an intersecting wall to where Leroux was digging. Since the wall to which I measured in Leroux's office continues through to become that wall over there in your office, I compared distances. It wasn't hard because you have a floor with twelve inch tiles. At any rate, I was surprised to find that the place he was trying to get through the wall was actually three feet *beyond* the back of the safe."

"What?" said Vickers, in spite of himself.

"Now, it's possible he miscalculated, of course," Max continued. "But if you consider the lengths he went to do this, it's hard to imagine he didn't calculate the place he was digging with great care. No, I think there was no mistake; he was exactly where he intended to be."

"Behind the safe," said Allison, "in the wall?"

"Not in the wall," said Max, shaking his head. "The safe was placed in an old brick enclosure that was originally for chimneys from the lower floors. But the chase, according to the drawing on the wall over there, was about ten feet long, leaving an empty but enclosed space almost five feet long behind the safe."

"And whatever Leroux wanted is in there?" said Vickers.

"That's right."

"This is all nonsense, Max," said Stilwell, angrily. "It's all guesswork and assumptions. You're stuck in the case, so you're desperately speculating, hoping for a miracle. I've bent over backwards to cooperate, and this is what I get...a damned fishing expedition with me as the fish. I suppose you now expect me to let you knock holes in my walls searching for buried treasure, or gold bars, or the crown jewels, or whatever you're guessing is in there besides rubble. Well, I won't have it! Enough is enough. I'll thank all of you to leave my private property right now. Come back when you have a warrant, or, better still, don't come back at all!"

Vickers and Allison slowly rose from their chairs. Allison looked pleadingly at Max, but Max didn't move. The bluff had failed and it was all coming apart, she thought. Poor Max. He played with fire and got burned.

Stilwell walked over to Max. "Did you hear me? You have no authority here. I want you off my property now!"

Max looked at him calmly. "I'm not guessing, Mr. Stilwell," he said in a calm, even voice. "I know exactly what is in there, and why it can't stay there any longer. I think it would be best if you were part of the solution rather than a hindrance. I will tell you what is in there."

Max leaned over and said something too soft for Allison and Vickers to hear. A remarkable change came over Stilwell. His anger drained away, then he stiffened and went pale. His eyes widened and he stared at Max.

"How do you...."

"Does it matter?" said Max. "The point is, I know."

Glenn Stilwell looked wilted. He slumped in his chair behind the desk and mumbled to himself. "Just a few more months. That's all I needed. Just a few more months..."

Max motioned towards the safe. "May I?"

Stilwell didn't look up, but waved a hand.

Max stepped into the safe. It was just as he remembered it. There were mostly empty shelves on each side and sheet metal walls all around. He pointed to a metal plate, about two feet wide by four high, screwed into the rear wall.

"I noticed this plate in the back the last time, but I assumed it was some sort of emergency escape in case someone got locked in. I understand the Diebold Company uses some device like that, but that plate is actually an access panel. Do you have a Phillips screwdriver handy, Mr. Stilwell?"

"There's one on the top shelf on the left."

"Yes; here it is." Max got the screwdriver and set to work. The panel had only six screws and they came out easily. Max pulled the panel and it came out with a metallic clang.

"Allison, Tom; you might want to have a look at this." They stood at the doorway of the safe peering in the exposed space.

The space beyond was inky black.

"Do you have a light, Mr. Stilwell?"

Stilwell was still slumped in his chair mumbling to himself, but he sat up.

"A light? Oh, yes. Of course." He reached for a small switch under the desk and flipped it. A light came on in the space. Allison and Vickers stood transfixed.

"Well, I'll be damned," said Vickers.

"Oh, Max," said Allison in a whisper. "It's breathtaking."

Max looked in, then turned back to Allison and Vickers.

"Allison, Tom; allow me to present the *Smiling Angel of Reims*."

*John Reisinger*

## Chapter 19
## The angel

For a few seconds, no one spoke. They just stood and stared.

"My God, Max. That's the most beautiful thing I've ever seen," said Vickers.

"It's stunning" said Allison. "It seems to glow with some holy inner light. That picture in the art book doesn't come close."

"It looks like you set up a little private display, Glenn," said Max.

"I treated it with the reverence it deserves," Stilwell replied. "I even have a concealed ventilation system so the humidity is kept down."

"Very nice," said Max. "Tom, will you help me get the painting out of there and into the room?"

"Sure, Max," said the chief, coming forward.

If anything, the *Smiling Angel of Reims* was even more stunning in the natural light. The angel seemed to be alive, and gracing them all with her approval for rescuing her from the darkness. Her robes flowed with a warm bluish hue, and seemed to rustle in some unseen breeze. The angel herself was radiant with an inner light.

John Reisinger

The gold frame was clearly much newer, but was overshadowed by the picture itself.

Max, Allison and the chief just stood looking at it from all angles and marveling at what they were experiencing.

"Just a few more months," said Stilwell, shaking his head. "I was going to return it to Reims on the tenth anniversary of the day it was shelled. It was to be my gift to the people of France."

"But...you stole it," Allison pointed out.

"No! I saved it!" Stilwell, who had been defeated and listless, suddenly sprang to life. "It would have been ashes if not for me. I was on an inspection tour one night and pulled into Reims. Just when I was passing the cathedral, the Germans started shelling. Everyone disappeared from the streets and I was standing there exposed. I could hear the shells coming. They make a whistling sound like banshees of death. The first shell hit a block away, then they started getting closer, like a walking barrage. I ran in the cathedral for protection but the place was deserted. I found myself in a side chapel and saw the smiling angel. There were several candles still lit and she seemed to beckon to me. If you think it looks alive now, you should see it by candlelight. She seemed to be assuring me that I was safe, and I stood there mesmerized for a long while, just staring at her. But then a shell hit and part of the roof fell in. It somehow missed me completely except for some dust, but the shell started a fire among the pews and choir stalls. Then part of the wall collapsed and I turned to get out of there. Something told me to look back and I did. The place was an inferno. The angel was gone!"

"Gone? Gone where?" said Allison, who by now was hanging on every word.

"Buried under the rubble. I just saw a corner of the frame sticking out and the corner was on fire! I couldn't leave it there, so I went back in and started digging the angel out. I beat out the fire on the frame, and slowly was able to get enough rubble cleared away to expose the entire painting. I tell you, in the light from the fire, she seemed to be pleading with me. Well, I couldn't let her be burned, but I couldn't free one corner of the frame that was being crushed beneath a big stone. The flames were getting hotter, so I took out my penknife and cut the picture out of the frame, rolled it up, and put it under my coat. I barely made it out before some more rubble buried the remaining frame. The next day, French authorities found the part of the frame that had been held under the heavy stone, and assumed the fire had destroyed the rest, including the painting."

"Why didn't you return it?" Max asked.

"I wanted to," said Stilwell, "but the country was in such chaos, I didn't think it would be safe. Between the battles, the artillery, and the Zeppelin bombing raids, the painting could have been destroyed any moment if it remained in France, so I packed it in a wooden box and sent it home via diplomatic courier. That sort of mail isn't examined by either a censor or customs, you know. I kept it a secret, even from Jacqueline. I couldn't display it at Casa Leone and keep it a secret, so I created a secure but concealed place when I renovated the building."

"Then why not return it after the war was over?" Max asked.

"I intended to, but there was always a reason not to. For several years, the cathedral hadn't been restored enough to properly house the painting, and I was afraid they'd put it in a museum somewhere, or, worse still, in

225

storage. So I held on to it and decided I would return it on the ten year anniversary of the day it was thought destroyed. That would be in about eight months."

"A likely story," said Vickers.

"It's true," said Stilwell. "My attorney has a sealed letter I left with him years ago with instructions to open it next year if anything happened to me. In it I told the whole story and spelled out my promise to return the painting as I said."

"How did Leroux find out you had it and where you kept it?" Vickers asked.

"I don't really know. He's French. Maybe someone saw me that night and told him."

"Mrs. Leroux might be able to clear that up," said Max. "Meanwhile, Mr. Stilwell, I'm afraid you have bigger problems than mere art theft."

"I'm way ahead of you, Max," said Vickers. "Mr. Glenn Stilwell, you are under arrest for the murder of Charles Leroux."

Stilwell; looked up. "Murder?"

"It's clear what happened," Vickers continued. "Leroux found out about the painting. We can't say just how yet, but somehow he did. He started boring through the wall to get to it and take it himself. Maybe he was a French patriot, or maybe he wanted to sell it on the black market. Either way, he was determined to get it. You found out. Maybe you were here one night, heard him and discovered what he was doing. You were facing losing the painting and being branded an art thief in the process. You couldn't face it, so you got your gun from the safe and killed him. You figured you could repair the wall once everything settled down and no one would ever guess the real reason for the killing. I expect you rigged the locked room trick as a further way of confusing the investigation. As owner of the building you know all the ins and out of the door locks. It probably wasn't too difficult."

"What? No! I admit taking the painting, but I didn't kill anyone," Stilwell sputtered.

"Now, Mr. Stilwell," the chief continued, "I can get a couple of my boys over here with the Paddy wagon and take you in in handcuffs, or you can agree to accompany me back to police headquarters voluntarily with a minimum of fuss and possible sensation."

Stilwell was quiet a moment, then shrugged. "Have it your way. I'll come along with you, but I want to call my attorney first."

Vickers motioned towards the phone. "Certainly. I'll wait."

"While Stilwell talked to his attorney on the telephone, Vickers turned to Max.

"Well, you've done it again, Max," said Vickers. "I don't know how you knew that painting would be in there, but it was. You and Allison saved the day. Without you two, we'd be drowning in false clues and sensational newspaper stories."

"Well..."

"All right. I'm ready," said Stilwell. "My attorney will meet us at the police headquarters before I answer any more questions."

"I think there will be less fuss if as few people go as possible," said Max. "Besides, Allison and I have an appointment at the Avon."

Glenn Stilwell nodded. "I agree. Max, I don't know how you figured it out, but you did. You were right about the painting, but I'm telling you all that I didn't kill Leroux. I didn't even know he was after the painting until ten minutes ago."

"We'll get all that sorted out," said Vickers. "Come along now."

"Chief," said Allison. "You might want to send an officer over to guard this office."

"Oh, right. Will do."


Max and Allison stepped out onto the sidewalk and the late afternoon shadows. Allison grabbed his arm.

"My hero!"

"Aw, shucks," said Max.

"So how did you know the painting that was supposed to be destroyed was actually in a cubbyhole behind Stilwell's safe?"

"I didn't know for sure, but it seemed likely."

"Maybe to you...."

"It all comes back to the art book. The book alone didn't mean much, but then I found out he was using it to apparently track down a specific painting. I knew Leroux was asking about the painting in case it was at Casa Leone. That's why he was chatting up Violet the maid. Why he thought the Stilwells had it in the first place I have no idea, but maybe Mrs. Leroux can enlighten us. When he figured out the painting wasn't at Casa Leone, Leroux must have deduced it was in a secure place where Glenn Stilwell would have access to it, but no one else would. When Leroux met with Stilwell, pretending to be a prospective tenant, he saw the floor plan in Stilwell's office and saw that the safe, which Stilwell kept open, was too small for the brick enclosure in which it was located, he saw his chance. He rented the adjacent office, set up a cover business, and set to work. But he was murdered before he got finished."

"Because Glenn Stilwell found out and killed him," said Allison. "A great piece of detection, and Glenn Stilwell will soon be on trial for murder, but you don't look as happy as I would have guessed."

"Oh, it's nothing; just another one of those loose ends."

"Now what?"

"Never mind," said Max. "Here we are at the Avon. It's just striking four and the elusive Mrs. Leroux awaits."

Marie Leroux was a dark haired woman, fashionably dressed and poised as if visiting an embassy. She received Max and Allison in her room for privacy and confidentiality. They sat comfortably in her small suite.

"Mrs. Leroux, I appreciate you talking to us," Max started off. "I think you should know that the police have just made an arrest, a local man who had the painting in his possession."

Mrs. Leroux shook her head. "So Charles was right. I am grateful that justice will be done, but it is too late for poor Charles."

"Mrs. Leroux, why was Charles looking for a painting that everyone said had been destroyed?"

"I asked him that, myself, many times," she answered. "It was a mission with him, an obsession."

"Could you tell us about it?" Allison asked.

She sighed, lit a cigarette, and leaned back in her chair. She took a deep drag, then exhaled slowly.

"Charles came from a wealthy family near Paris. We were engaged to be married when the war came and the *Boche* invaded France. Charles enlisted as a common *Poilu*, or foot soldier, and won a battlefield commission at the Marne in 1914. In 1917 he was with his unit, the 743rd, near Reims. One day, on leave, he stopped at the cathedral and saw the smiling angel. He was so struck by her, that he prayed for both France and for his own safety. Every chance he got, he returned to the chapel and prayed to the smiling angel. He was in many battles, but miraculously, was never wounded. Sometimes men on either side of him fell, but Charles was untouched."

She paused. "Until the day he died, he believed the angel watched over him and protected him. Perhaps that is why he felt the need to rescue her."

"One night," she continued, "the *Boche* shelled Reims. They hit the cathedral and the angel was destroyed. Charles was devastated and fought like a madman for revenge. After the war, he heard a rumor that the angel had somehow survived. Charles became obsessed with the idea. He spent his time in old archives, and in interviewing people who lived in Reims at the time. Finally, he talked to an old lady who said she saw a man in a brown uniform running from the cathedral that night with something rolled up under his arm. That was all she knew, but a brown uniform had to be either British or American. The French wore *bleu horizon* , or light blue, and the Germans *feldgrau,* or grayish-green. So Charles checked with the embassies and the military records to track down who might have been in the area that night. It took him years, but finally, he found a record of American Embassy people visiting areas in the war zones and found that a Major Glenn Stilwell had been in Reims that night and went home not long afterwards."

"So he followed Glenn Stilwell to Maryland?" Max asked.

"Not right away. He was afraid the American might have sold the painting to an unscrupulous collector, so we moved to Philadelphia, so he could be close to Washington, D.C., Baltimore, Philadelphia, New York, and Boston, where wealthy collectors and galleries were most likely to be. He spent a year haunting art galleries and auction houses all over the East Coast, but no one had seen the angel. There were some forgeries on the market, but they only fooled the *nouveau riche*, not the serious collectors. That meant that this Mr. Stilwell still had the angel in his possession."

"So your husband decided to go to Easton and track it down?" Max asked.

"Yes, and that was where I drew the line. We had traveled all over France on his quest, and then to Philadelphia, and now to rural Maryland? We had been quarreling for some time about how he was obsessed and thought of nothing else, so we agreed to separate and consider a divorce. I told him his obsession wasn't healthy, that it was dangerous. I warned him it would destroy him in the end. Now he's gone."

She was silent a while. Max and Allison looked at each other, but said nothing.

"The man the police arrested; he was this Stilwell, perhaps?"

"Yes," said Max. "The police believe he caught your husband trying to break in to where the painting was kept, and killed him."

"*Qu'elle dommage.* I told him....I told him so many times. But he said he'd rather die than allow the angel to disappear forever."

"For what it's worth, Mrs. Leroux," said Allison in a soft voice, "your husband's efforts resulted in the angel being found. It will be returned to France. I think that was his wish."

"Yes," said Mrs. Leroux, "he got his wish."

## Chapter 20

## More questions

After their interview with Marie Leroux, Max and Allison sat in the lobby of the Avon Hotel quietly discussing the day's events.

"Poor Mrs. Leroux. Her husband found what he was looking for and got murdered as a result. She was right about it ending badly for him."

"Yes," said Max. "He found the angel, but lost his life."

"So now what happens?"

Max shrugged. "The usual, I guess. A media storm, lots of wagging tongues, and a trial for Glenn Stilwell."

"All right, Max. What gives? You said there was a loose end; something that's still bothering you. What is it?"

Max frowned. "The painting. Why was it there?"

"You should be thankful it was. Otherwise, you'd have enough egg on your face to serve breakfast to everyone in Easton."

"But why was it there? I don't mean why did Glenn Stilwell put it there in the first place; that's clear enough. I want to know why was it *still* there today? Why didn't he move it somewhere else?"

Allison looked at him. "Yes, of course. I see what you mean. If he knew Leroux had discovered the hiding place, why didn't he move the painting somewhere else?"

"Exactly. He had to have known there was a chance someone would look behind that chalkboard, discover what Leroux was doing, and figure out why he was doing it. It's been days, but Stilwell left the *angel* right where it was; right where someone might find it just the way I did. Why?"

"Nobody but you would have figured out what was in there, Max."

"Maybe they wouldn't have known about the *angel*, but they would have figured something valuable was there. The police might have even gotten a search warrant and discovered the *angel*. Then Glenn Stilwell would have killed Leroux for nothing. He had to have realized that."

"Well, clearly he didn't. People do irrational things under pressure."

"I suppose so, but still... Say, I think it wouldn't hurt to get an expert opinion."

"What, a psychiatrist?"

"No. Wait here a minute." Max went to the front desk and returned a few seconds later.

"Good. He's in. The desk clerk is sending for him now."

"Sending for whom?"

"An expert, of course."

"What ho, Max, and the lovely Allison! How delightful!" came a voice from behind them.

"Oh; Mr. Smith..."

"Smythe-Cunningham, but please call me Nigel, Allison."

"Right. Uh, Max, may I speak to you for a moment?" She took him aside.

"Why are you getting him involved?"

"I'm checking something. We're going back to Stilwell's office."

A few minutes later, Max, Allison, and Smythe-Cunningham arrived at Stilwell's office. By this time, a police guard had been posted, but the painting was still there.

"Oh, I say; this *is* a mystery," said Smythe-Cunningham, rubbing his hands together in anticipation. "Very cryptic, don't you know, like the big scene in *Tower of Death*, by Emily Marshall. Now what did you want me to see?"

"This," said Max, stepping from in front of the painting.

Smythe-Cunningham was momentarily stunned. "Surely that can't be..."

"It is," said Max. "I will explain how it got here in a minute, but first, I would like you to authenticate it so there is no doubt. You're the only person in Easton capable."

Smythe-Cunningham walked around the painting reverently. "Stunning. I've never seen it in the flesh, of course, but the reproductions do not do it justice. May I have a closer look?"

"Of course." Max explained briefly, how the painting was saved and brought to the United States, and Leroux's efforts to obtain it.

"I say, Max. You were right all along, old boy. The art book was the key to the entire case. Why, Agatha Christie couldn't have cooked up a more clever plot. I'm sorry, but I'm still astonished."

He reached into an inside coat pocket and took out a pair of white gloves and a magnifying glass and carefully examined the entire surface front and back. "Well, of course, it's been remounted in a modern day frame, but that's perfectly consistent with the story."

Smythe-Cunningham then took out a pair of forceps and delicately raised several loose threads and wrinkled sections of the canvas for closer examination. He even sniffed the surfaces like a bloodhound on the scent. Allison and Max looked at each other.

"An expert at work," Allison whispered.

Finally, Nigel sat back in a nearby chair, still staring at the painting.

"Extraordinary, quite extraordinary," he kept mumbling.

"Well," said Max, "what is your professional opinion?"

The art expert looked at Max. "You know, Max, I am dashed glad you've given me the chance to be of some utility in a real-life murder case..."

"Sure, sure, but what do you think?"

"...and I would never want to disappoint you..."

Max raised his eyebrows. "But?"

"Well, the fact is, I can't be 100 percent certain, but I believe this is a copy."

"You mean a fake?"

Smythe-Cunningham looked both flustered and embarrassed. "I can't speculate on the motives of whoever is responsible, but I do believe this is not the original. Dash it all, I'm as sorry as you are, Max. The art world would love for something like the *Smiling Angel* to resurface, but...well I think whoever did this is extraordinarily talented. I confess, I've never seen anything this good that wasn't painted by one of the old masters. This work is absolutely splendid. In its own way, this is a masterpiece, no matter who painted it."

Allison sat in another chair, shaking her head. "So how do you know?"

"Well," said Smythe-Cunningham reluctantly, "the type of paints and glazes that were used in the early 1500s were crude by today's standards, and far more delicate. If this painting had been in a fire severe enough to char part of the frame, I would expect sections of it to be blackened, maybe even cracked, but the paint looks fine. There is some blackening on the canvas backing, but I can't tell if its soot or paint. Plus, the brush strokes look as if there has been some overpainting and layering, something a forger would have to do to recreate rather than create fresh. The weave of the canvas looks a bit coarse to me as well, but I can't be certain without a microscope. Also, a canvas that has been rolled up tightly will sometimes show cracks in the surface, although that isn't certain. No, Max. I'm sorry, but all in all, I have serious doubts about the authenticity of this painting."

Smythe-Cunningham shrugged apologetically.

Max nodded. "Well, I asked for your opinion, and that's what I got. Thank you."

"So I guess that shoots your theory of the case, Max," said Allison.

"On the contrary, I think it vindicates it."

"What?"

"We'll discuss it later. We've taken up too much of Nigel's time already."


Max was unusually quiet at home that night. Allison knew from long experience that Max's brooding moments meant that he was trying to fit a piece into a puzzle that was being reluctant to accept it.

"Max," she said finally, "Just tell me one thing; is the angel a fake? And if it is, why all this trouble for a copy?"

"That's two things," said Max, smiling.

"Indulge a mother-to-be."

"I think a better pair of questions would be why would Leroux and Stilwell expend all that time and energy on a fake, but if it is genuine, why would Smythe-Cunningham think it wasn't? I need one more piece of evidence to be sure of the answer."

"So where do you expect to find it?" said Allison.

"At the moment, my dear, I really don't know if it even exists."

"Well, that's encouraging."

She was silent another minute before speaking again. "So is Glenn Stilwell guilty?"

"Of snatching the painting? Almost certainly. You heard his confession."

"You know what I mean; guilty of murdering Charles Leroux."

"That will be up to a jury. I'm just trying to make sure all the evidence is consistent and complete before that happens. At the moment, I don't think it is."

Allison sighed. "In the meantime, I think tomorrow's press briefing will be a lively one."


Jacqueline Stilwell called the Hurlock house at seven that night, demanding to know why Glenn had been arrested and why Max hadn't stopped it.

"Mrs. Stilwell, I have to uncover the evidence as best I can. Your husband had a strong motive and not much of an alibi."

"A lot of nonsense! I know the press boys are breathing down your neck, but you got the wrong man."

"Well, Mrs. Stilwell, the investigation is still going on. There are a lot of loose ends to consider."

"Just make sure one of those loose ends isn't the end of a rope!" she snapped, and hung up.

"Too bad," said Allison. "She was just starting to like you. Oh, there goes the phone again. This will be socko night."

"I have to call Vickers after this call and tell him about Smythe-Cunningham's evaluation of the painting."

Allison picked up the phone. "Hello? Oh, yes he's here."

John Reisinger

"No need to call the chief," said Allison, "Here he is."

"Max!" came the voice of Chief Vickers on the line, "The word is out about arresting Glenn Stilwell. Al White and Bob Avery were hanging around police headquarters when I got back with Stilwell in hand. I didn't answer any questions, but it was obvious we were arresting him. It'll be in all the papers tomorrow. On top of that, Stilwell's attorney is stirring up a fuss. He's threatening to petition the court for a writ of *habeus corpus*."

"I think that's just a ploy," said Max. "As far as I know, that would only apply if the arrest was unlawful."

"He claims there is no proof the painting was stolen, and in fact, no proof that the painting is even genuine."

"Well," admitted Max, "He might have a point on the genuine part. I took Nigel Smythe-Cunningham over to inspect the painting and he seems to think it's a copy."

"A what? Max I've got ten years more till retirement. I don't need this. So where does that leave us? Up the creek?"

"Well, it's just one man's opinion..."

"One man who happens to be an authority!"

"Yes, well, I think we're going to need more evidence. It's possible that even if the painting is a fake, Glenn Stilwell thought it was genuine and killed Leroux just as we thought."

"Well, I have to meet with the mayor tomorrow morning, and I have to know what to tell him. We'll get crucified if we arrested Glenn Stilwell based on a fake painting."

The line went dead.

Max looked at Allison, who was looking both worried and sympathetic.

"Well," he said, "you won't have to worry about me running off to solve any more murder cases after junior comes into this world. The way this case is going, it's very unlikely I'll ever be asked again."

*John Reisinger*

# Chapter 21
# Time running out

ARREST IN BUCKET SHOP CASE

*Wealthy local Glenn Stilwell in Easton Jail*

*Long-lost painting said to be motive*

Max  shook his head as he read the headline the next day. He wasn't surprised.

"Max!" Vickers called to him as he stepped in the door.

"Morning, Tom, how's..."

"Stilwell's lawyer just got him released on bail, effective at two this afternoon. If we're going to question him again, we'd better do it soon."

"Max! Chief! How did you catch Stilwell? Is he dangerous?"

Several reporters called out from the doorway.

"More reporters?" said Max.

"The news travels fast and people are gathering from all over."

"Well, it looks like Stilwell's release and the press briefing will be held at the same time," Max observed. "Should be interesting."

"Interesting? Are you kidding? It's a necktie party and I'm the guest of honor."

"Now, Tom. It's not as bad as all that," said Max.

"It's worse. I had a little revival session with the mayor a short while ago. He wants to hold a meeting at one o'clock to go over the evidence before the press briefing at two. He wants all the other suspects there in case any of them have something to add or dispute, and he wants that art guy there to tell us why the picture is a fake..."

"He said copy, not necessarily fake."

The chief continued. "It's almost like the old mystery cliché of gathering the suspects together and revealing the murderer, except we've already revealed the murderer. This is just to make sure there's no last minute facts, discoveries, or confessions to derail the whole investigation. There will be too many people watching to risk that."

Max nodded. "And with Glenn Stilwell out on bail until the trial, there will be plenty of time to run down any late discoveries."

"Right. He wants Allison and Mrs. Leroux there as well; Allison, so she'll be prepared for the press briefing, and Mrs. Leroux so she'll be on board and not give any interviews to the press telling them we're all wet about who killed her husband."

"Makes sense. The mayor is a politician, after all."

"...and he wants me to hand the meeting over to you to put it all together and assess where we stand and what can be released to the press boys at two."

"Also a smart move," said Max. "That way, if things come unglued, I'll get the blame."

"Well..."

"Never mind, I think the Stilwells need to be there as well," said Max.

"All right, Max. I'll get my boys to round them up. We'll tell them they are wanted there to provide any information they might have. That'll get them there without feeling threatened. The reporters will notice and howl, but they'll get their chance at two. So, if you're going to get that last bit of evidence to convict Stilwell, Max, you'd better do it fast."

"I intend to, Tom. I stopped by Chesapeake Investments on the way in and looked it over once more."

"Did you find any more paintings I should know about?" said Vickers, bitterly. "Maybe Stilwell grabbed the Mona Lisa while he was at it?"

"No, but I looked at the desk. It was very interesting."

"The desk? Holy cats, Max. Are you off your rocker, too?"

"Tom. I want to look through the evidence in those boxes once again."

"We've been over it a hundred times. Most of it's just piles of old stock slips."

"I know, but I'd like to look at it all just the same."

"Fine," said Vickers. "If you need me, I'll be reading the help wanted ads."

The back room was cool and quieter than the front, but was visible through a glass panel so there was less chance of anyone tampering with the evidence. Max got the three boxes, placed them on the table and started withdrawing envelopes. There were photos, but he skipped over them.

Max leaned back in the chair and looked up to find Allison standing in the doorway.

"Tom said you were in here, Max. Have you found a smoking gun, yet?"

Max shook his head. "Not yet...that is, assuming it exists."

"Do you think there's enough evidence against Glenn Stilwell already?"

"Not for me, but I'm not a jury."

"Max, are you all right?"

"I was about to ask you the same question, Allison. You look tired and distracted."

"That's only because I'm tired and distracted," she replied, laughing ironically. "I'm tired of dealing with people who demand more than I can give them. I'm tired of people acting as if they are concerned about one thing when they really care about something entirely different. Well, that's human nature, I suppose. I have to get going. Good luck, Max. See you at one."

Max kissed her, then watched her go, but her words kept rattling around in his head. "People acting as if they cared about one thing when they really care about something entirely different."

Max put another long distance call through to the director of the Metropolitan Museum of Art in New York.

"Hello; this is Max Hurlock calling about the Bucket Shop Murder down in Maryland. There have been some interesting developments since we spoke. If you have a minute of two, I have a few follow up questions that could be very important."

"Yes, Mr. Hurlock, I'll put Mr. Robinson right on."

"Hello again, Mr. Robinson. There's been an interesting development in the Bucket Shop murder down here in Maryland. It seems Leroux was looking for the *Smiling Angel of Reims,* and it seems he found it."

"What? But how in the world...?"

Max told Robinson the whole story and began asking questions. Afterwards, Max attacked the evidence boxes with renewed energy.


Allison, meanwhile, was on her way to police headquarters to see if there was anything new she should know before the upcoming press briefing.

"Allison!" She turned and saw Chip Carswell advancing on her. Had she made a list of people she was most anxious to see that morning, Chip Carswell would probably be near the bottom.

"What's this about a big meeting this afternoon? I hear the press is excluded. What gives?"

"The mayor wants the people involved in the case to meet and review the evidence to assure all the bases are covered."

"Without the press?"

"Of course without the press. If too many details of the evidence leak out, it might compromise any trial that results."

"Can't you give me a hint, Allison?"

"Sorry, Chip, but I promise you you'll know as soon as everyone else does."

"Allison, I'm a reporter. I need to know *before* everyone else does!"

"All I can predict, Chip, is things will be hopping in old Easton Town this afternoon."

## Chapter 22
## Putting the pieces together

With a knot of reporters milling around outside police headquarters, Max, Allison, Chief Vickers, Glenn and Jacqueline Stilwell, Ned Gunther the estate manager, Mrs. Leroux, Marsha Tolliver, Grayson Dunlop, and Nigel Smythe-Cunningham faced off uneasily in the lunchroom of Easton Police Headquarters. In one corner, Max stood in whispered conversation with Chief Vickers, who looked confused and exasperated.

"Are you sure about all this, Max?"

"Just follow along, Tom. It'll be fine I promise."

A sergeant brought some glasses of water, and the chief brought the meeting to order.

"I want to thank all you folks for being here," he began.

"You didn't give us much choice," muttered Dunlop.

"We wanted to get all the involved people together to compare notes in case there's something in all the testimony or evidence we've overlooked, and to let you all know where we are. As you may know, we've made an arrest, but have brought no formal charges as yet. I'm going to turn the meeting over to Max Hurlock to review the evidence."

Max stood up and looked over the room. Marsha Tolley exhibited mild curiosity, and Grayson Dunlop looked bored. Marie Leroux looked gloomy and the Stilwell party looked indignant. Only Nigel Smythe-Cunningham, finally participating in a real-life mystery, seemed to be enjoying his moment in the spotlight.

"Charles Leroux," Max began, "came to America, and to Easton on a mission; to track down the *Smiling Angel of Reims,* a priceless painting thought to have been destroyed in the war. Through a lot of detective work both in France and in the states, he believed, correctly as it turns out, that the painting was secretly in the possession of Mr. Stilwell, who had rescued the painting in a bombing raid, but had then failed to return it. Leroux's problem was finding exactly where the painting was kept so he could recover it for France. To that end, he became friendly with Marsha Tolley to find out where the Stilwells lived and owned property where the painting might be kept. He later became friendly with Violet McGuinn to find out if the painting was at Casa Leone. It wasn't."

"Of course not," Jacqueline Stilwell muttered.

"Through some pretty impressive detective work," Max continued, "Leroux came to believe the painting was in the Stilwell Building behind Stilwell's safe in an old brick chimney space. Seeing the adjacent space was for rent, Leroux set up Chesapeake Investments and worked nights chipping his way through the brick wall to find his treasure. He no doubt intended to rebrick the wall afterwards so that it might be weeks before anyone noticed the painting was gone."

The grumbling was silent now, as everyone leaned forward to hear the story.

"I don't know how long it took him, but finally the day came when he planned to break through the wall as soon as everyone else went home. At this point, it appeared that Glenn Stilwell might have gotten wind of the plan and shot Leroux to protect his painting..."

The Stilwells began to object, but Max raised a hand to silence them,

"But there was one problem with this scenario; we couldn't figure out why Mr. Stilwell, having killed Mr. Leroux, wouldn't have moved the painting to a safer place until the heat was off. But he never did and we finally figured out why. It was obvious; he didn't move the painting because he didn't know what Leroux was doing until the police found the painting *after* the murder."

"Wait!" exclaimed Glenn Stilwell. "That proves I didn't kill Leroux."

Max ignored him and continued. "So the day of the murder, Charles Leroux was finally ready to break through the wall and was free to find the painting unhindered by Mr. Stilwell or anyone else. Then fate intervened. On the street that day, Leroux ran into a fellow art enthusiast, someone he had met months earlier as he canvassed the art galleries in his efforts to locate the painting. The news was too exciting not to share with one of the few people who would really appreciate it, so he told his friend everything and invited him to stop by that night for the great moment when he would break through the wall and find the painting."

The people in the room sat silent, looking confused. Max proceeded.

"That night, after everyone else had gone, the friend returned as promised to view the great moment. Leroux removed a single brick and probably shone a flashlight into the dark space beyond, like Harold Carter discovering the tomb of Tutankhamun a few years ago. At that moment, both men knew that the *Smiling Angel of Reims* had been found. It must have been a wonderful moment for Charles Leroux, the culmination of his quest. He had been right all along; the angel had survived and was in the possession of Glenn Stilwell.

"But unfortunately for Charles Leroux, the friend was more than just an art enthusiast; he was also in the business of selling forgeries to wealthy but gullible collectors who relished the idea of owning a great work of art that the rest of the world mistakenly thought had been destroyed. What's more, the friend had secretly sold several forgeries of the angel to these men. Some of these collectors were no doubt newly rich organized crime bosses who would not take kindly to being duped, and once the real *Smiling Angel of Reims* surfaced, the deception would be obvious. The friend could not take the chance of being exposed and the target of retribution by his cheated customers. The *Smiling Angel* had to remain hidden.

"So the friend shot Charles Leroux and replaced the last brick that had been removed. The new mortar was obvious. Then he covered up the area with the chalkboard, cleaned and dried the tools, and made his way out of the office. That was when he locked the door to confuse the police."

"How did he do that?" Grayson Dunlop suddenly wasn't as bored as before.

"The key is the old fashioned type and is quite loose in the keyhole. The friend simply placed the key in the lock on the inside, closed the door behind him, then inserted a pair of forceps in the keyhole to grasp the key by the shaft and turn it, locking the door. The key in the evidence box is quite clearly scratched in that area."

Max turned to Smythe-Cunningham. "Nigel, why don't you show them the forceps you carry to examine art works, so they can see what I mean."

Smythe-Cunningham looked ashen. "Oh, I say, old top. You're never accusing *me*, are you?"

"Very good, Nigel. You really *are* good at mysteries," said Max. Marie Leroux started to rise to her feet.

"This man killed my husband?"

The light was dawning in the eyes of the Stilwell party as well. "And I went through all this or nothing?" said Glenn.

"Well," said Max, "you still have to explain to the authorities where you got that painting and why you didn't give it back, but you didn't kill anyone."

Smythe-Cunningham was regaining has composure. "Well, I must say, Max, you and the local constabulary have certainly taken the conventions of the mystery genre to heart. You have a room full of suspects and an unexpected shocking twist worthy of Agatha Christie herself to expose the unlikely killer. It would make a splendid story, no doubt, but I'm afraid this is the real world and the courts do rather insist on proof. As near as I can see, that is in short supply. In fact, there is absolutely nothing connecting me with Leroux or placing me in his office the night of the murder. I must say, I'm rather disappointed in you. You did a splendid job of sniffing out the painting, of course, but as far as convicting anyone of the crime, it seems you've come a cropper as we say in Old Blighty."

Max ignored him and continued. "I first thought you had something to hide when I noticed you had newly shaved off your mustache. Now I realize it was so anyone who might have seen you when you ran into Leroux in the street would have a harder time identifying you. I also noticed that you consistently downplayed the possibility of a painting being involved in the case. You were very convincing, too. Even after the painting had been found, you tried to convince us it was a copy, to protect your forgeries. With art, as with medicine, though, it is often advisable to get a second opinion, and I went to the top; Edward Robinson, Director of the Metropolitan Museum of Art in New York. It seems that rumors of the survival of the *Smiling Angel* have been around for years, something you never told me when you were trying to convince me otherwise. I also learned of the brisk trade in stolen or forged artworks, and how the police have raided your gallery several times without success. They believe you have a stable of forgers turning out such things..."

"That's slander! I'll sue the bloody.."

"Oh, I didn't hear all that from him," said Max, calmly. "That came directly from several articles I found in the New York Times and those articles were based on the police reports. You've made quite a splash up there, Nigel."

"All very interesting in a circumstantial sort of way," said Smythe-Cunningham, "but it's still conjecture and guesswork. You still have no proof I was ever there."

Max went to a box on the table and took out the three files he had examined earlier. "Charles Leroux had an unusual filing system. He gave his customers stock slips to signify purchases, keeping a copy for himself, and recording it in a ledger. When the stock was sold, he stamped the slips Void, marked the book, and threw the old slips away. He did this each evening. We paired up the Void slips in the trash with entries in the ledger."

The people in the room looked at each other blankly at this sudden detour into bookkeeping. What could this have to do with a stolen painting?

"But here is the interesting part," Max continued. "Between the time a slip was Voided and entered into the ledger for the day, Leroux used the backs of them for note paper. If something happened he wanted to place in his journal, grocery lists, unusual phone calls, notes on what he needed to do the next day, etc, he would write it on the back of one of the voided slips and at the end of the day, enter the stock information in the ledger, and whatever notes he had made in the journal. Sort of a clumsy system, but it meant he didn't have to leave either the ledger or the journal out in plain view during office hours.

"Now the slips are preprinted with some legal boilerplate on the back about terms and conditions, all sales final, etc., so there isn't much room for anything else. As a result, Leroux wrote his notes in the margins in very small letters, so we all missed the notes at first, because we were concentrating on the stock transactions on the front. The notes were easy to miss because there were a lot of slips and most of them did not have any notes on the back at all. It was only this morning that the police methodically went through the notes and were able to match up every slip found in the trash with entries in the ledger and the journal."

Allison smiled quietly. She knew that what Max really meant was that *he* had matched up the information. She noticed that Vickers seemed in no hurry to set the record straight.

Max held up a stock slip. "Here is one of 15 slips voided on the day of the murder. As you can see, the tiny handwritten note on the back simply says 'breakthrough tonight!', the meaning of which should be obvious. Now here is another slip from the same day." He rustled through a pile of papers.

"Ah, here it is, a voided slip for ten shares of Amalgamated something-or-other, also dated the day of the murder. On the back....well, Chief Vickers, if you have your reading glasses, why don't you read it to the people?"

Chief Vickers took the paper and adjusted his glasses. "Let's see. It has the date and then says...

*'Ran into Smythe-Cunningham from gallery in NY. Told him of my discovery. He agreed to come to the office tonight at 8 to witness the breakthrough and authenticate the painting!'*"

"Thank you, chief," said Max. "Nigel, I think you probably checked his books before you left to be sure there was no reference to you in there and there wasn't, but you never thought to look in the slips in the drawer, or if you did, you didn't look carefully at the backs. Charles Leroux never entered these notes in the books that night because you killed him before he got the chance, but they're still plainly in writing. I believe that is the proof you mentioned?"

Smythe-Cunningham did not respond. Chief Vickers stood up.

"Nigel Smythe-Cunningham, I hereby arrest you for the murder of Charles Leroux. Come along. Mr. Stilwell has the cell all warmed up for you."

The room erupted into excited voices talking over each other. "Thank you for coming, Folks," said a sergeant escorting the crowd out of the building. "We apologize for the inconvenience."

Glenn Stilwell seemed to be in a daze, but Jacqueline Stilwell came up to Max and actually hugged him.

"You've done it again, Max. You saved a Stilwell from a murder rap at the hands of the Easton Police. We are very grateful."

She turned to Allison. "Allison, I should have known that Max had hidden depths. Otherwise, why would someone like you ever marry him?"

Allison grinned. "Well, he is handy around the house..."

Max tried to spread the credit to Chief Vickers, but everyone knew the real story, and everyone thanked Max and Allison profusely. When Vickers came back into the room, an embarrassed Max apologized.

"Max," said Vickers, "you and Allison saved my skin, and the mayor's, too. You deserve all the credit."

He turned to Allison. "Allison, the press boys are getting restless out there. Why don't you move that press briefing up a bit?"

"Sure thing," she replied, "as soon as we can get the room cleared."

## Chapter 23
## Summing up

As Max attempted to slip away, he passed the cells area and saw Smythe-Cunningham beckoning to him from behind the bars.

"Max! Over here! I want to speak to you."

Max went up to the cell. The bars were cold and covered with chipped gray paint.

"Good job, Max," Smythe-Cunningham began. "You found the fatal clue and put the pieces together just like S. S. Van Dine in *The Scarab Murder Case*."

"Are you admitting it?"

"Why not? I'm finished and I know it. You were right; that painting is the genuine article. Once certain of my clients find out, jail might be the safest place to be. "

"Wait a minute," said Max. "What happened to your accent?"

Smythe-Cunningham laughed. "Well, it appears the great gumshoe of the Eastern Shore didn't deduce everything after all. The accent was phony. I was born in New York. The accent was a put on to fool the rubes. My name isn't Nigel Smythe-Cunningham either, it's Nick Smith. I thought my name should be a bit more British to go with the accent. So Nick became Nigel, Smith became

Smythe, and because I consider myself a very devious actor, I added Cunningham for good measure. Get it? Cunning ham."

Max nodded. "I get it; cunning ham indeed. How did you get into all this?"

Smith sighed. "Mostly by accident. I was born in Brooklyn, dropped out of school and worked at a tailor shop next to a wealthy area, mostly doing cutting, ordering and bookkeeping. Well, one day a fellow came in with a couple of paintings he was trying to sell. A real desperate starving artist type. I talked the shop owner into displaying them and selling them on consignment. A month later, we actually sold one of the paintings when a customer asked about it and on a whim, I referred to the artist as someone who was 'newly discovered'. Of course the artist was overjoyed and said he could paint in all sorts of styles, so I asked him to paint different styles under different names. Soon, I had a dozen paintings by 'newly discovered' artists, the rich folks told their friends, and soon I was able to open my own gallery.

"Eventually, I got some other artists, including one who turned out to be an excellent forger. That's when Nigel Smythe-Cunningham came into existence to sell the high end goods. From there it was a short step to selling forgeries to people with more money than caution. Charles Leroux stopped by my gallery about a year ago asking about the *Smiling Angel*. Of course, if he'd been a collector, I might have tried to sell him a black market forgery with a good story, but I could see he was just an enthusiast, so I gave him the standard line that the thing was destroyed and I had no knowledge of it. Frankly, I had forgotten about it until I ran into him on the street here in Easton."

Smith got serious. "Look, Max. The thing is, I never meant to kill anyone. I went there that night hoping Leroux was wrong and that the angel wasn't there, but when he removed that brick and shone the flashlight inside and I saw that face in the light, I knew he had found it. I tried to talk him into leaving it alone; tried to convince him Stilwell had been taken in by a copy, but it was no use. Leroux was determined. I felt I had to kill him, or I'd be ruined and probably killed myself. I carry a small pistol for protection because of the high price artwork I deal with. Strictly illegal under the Sullivan Act, of course, but I'd rather be in jail than dead. Anyway, I killed him and now I'll be ruined anyway. You were right about my trying to mislead you. Pretty ironic, when you think about it."

"Ironic? How's that?" said Max.

"In the end, I was done in by an angel."

That night, Max and Allison stopped in St Michaels on their way home to pick up some groceries from Bemis's General Store, then came home for another meal of leftovers. For a long time, they ate in weary silence, then fortified with the food, began to talk again.

"So how was the press briefing?" said Max.

Allison stared out in space. "Oh, chaos in a very small place best describes it. There were two more reporters there. One was from the Inquirer. Everyone was yelling and tossing dumb questions. They almost seemed disappointed that Glenn Stilwell didn't do it."

Max nodded. "I suppose from their point of view, Stilwell as the murderer would have been a much better story; rich guy killing for stolen art treasure. I can see the headlines now."

"Yes, they acted like a dog whose bone had been taken away and replaced with a piece of Zwieback bread. They felt cheated."

"Truth is stranger than fiction but a lot less sensational sometimes."

Allison looked indignant. "Well, I for one think it's much better story. Just think; a romantic quest undone by a treacherous friend; a secret treasure vault; a locked door crime; and a dogged amateur detective who cuts through it all."

Max smiled. "I'd take a bow, but I'm too tired right now. We just can't seem to get away from murders."

"Well, that's because you keep solving them."

"Ah, so that's where we went wrong. Max and Allison save the day. Well, now we can get back to starting a family."

Allison smiled, then became thoughtful. "Max, having the baby won't, well, change us, will it?"

"Change us? Of course it will change us. There'll be another mouth to feed and another personality to contend with. Then there's school, and ..."

"I don't mean that," she interrupted. "I mean us. Will it change how we feel about each other?"

"Why should it? Are you planning on going crazy once you're a mother?"

"No; I just thought it might change things between us. You remember you once told me about the Ulrichs over in Denton? They had a baby and got divorced a year later."

"The Ulrichs," said Max, "couldn't stand each other even before they had the baby. They had the baby thinking it would bring them together and it didn't. They'd have been better off if they *had* changed, but they couldn't. You and I, on the other hand, are eminently compatible, and I continue to find you endlessly fascinating. No pint-sized screamer is going to change that."

"Oh, Max..."

"On the other hand, you do tend to worry about silly things..."

"All right. Quit while you're ahead, mister."

The telephone rang inside the house.

"Saved by the bell," said Max, standing up slowly. "I'll get it. If it's another murder, I'll say we're closed on account of pregnancy."

He returned a minute later.

"That was your friend Bob Avery, Bob on the job, as I believe he calls himself."

"Bob from the Sun? What did he want?"

"He wants to do a human interest article about you for something he called the brown section."

"The brown section? That's the slick photogravure supplement published every week as part of the Sunday Sun. You know, like the comics."

"Oh, so we'll be rubbing elbows with the Nebbs, the Bungle Family, the Toonerville Folks, Mutt and Jeff and the Gumps?"

"No, silly. The brown section is separate and always has lots of photos and human interest stories."

Max nodded. "Well, that explains it. He wants to do an article, with photos of the former Sun reporter who helps crack murder cases; the 'Tommy and Tuppence of the Eastern Shore', he called it."

"Ugh. Look, I like Bob and I'd like to help him in his career, but if he wants to write about us, he's got to drop the Tommy and Tuppence references."

"Well..."

"I mean, I know they're Agatha Christie characters and very clever and all that, but honestly, who calls an adult woman Tuppence? It's revolting! It makes her sound like a cocker spaniel."

"Anyway, Bob wants to do an interview. I didn't mention our trophies, but I suppose he'd like to see them as well. The question is, do we want him to do all this?"

Allison sighed. "Not especially, but one thing I learned from my skirmishes with reporters is that you can't kill a story by refusing to cooperate. That just piques their curiosity and they dig elsewhere. Besides, it'll be my chance to head off any references to Tuppence. So when does he want to do the interview?"

"Tomorrow. Maybe at ten or so."

"That's fine, but I'll have to check in with the mayor first. He's having a formal announcement of the arrest."

"I'll tell Bob."

Max was back a minute later and sat back down. "All set."

"So what will happen to your friend Mr. Smythe-Whatchamacallit?"

"He'll stand trial for murder, possibly second degree. After that, it's up to the jury."

"How about Glenn Stilwell?"

"Well, if his attorney can verify that he has an old letter from Glenn Stilwell committing to returning the painting voluntarily, and I have no doubt that he can, I expect not much will happen after that."

Allison nodded. "I was thinking the same thing. Technically, he stole a French national treasure, but he also saved it from destruction, protected it, and was making plans to return it. I expect they'll be so glad to get the painting back, they'll think Glenn Stilwell is a hero."

"And thanks to you," said Max, "the mayor and the Easton Police are going to look pretty good."

"Thanks to both of us. Still, I expect they'll hog the credit and tell us to take a walk."

"Well, discretion is one reason they asked us to help," Max reminded her.

"And we've been discrete," she retorted. "The articles have been good; I haven't blabbed; and you stayed in the background even though you had the breakthrough that solved the case. They couldn't ask for much more. I think a public thank you is the least they could do."

"I'm sure Tom Vickers and the mayor will be grateful."

"Not publicly, they won't be," said Allison. "You just watch. They begged you to save them, but now, they'll pretend you don't exist."

The next morning, when Max and Allison arrived in Easton, the headlines were as breathless as ever.

FORGERY RING BEHIND BUCKET SHOP MURDER

SURPRISE KILLER IN BUCKET SHOP CASE

POLICE ARREST ART DEALER IN LOCKED ROOM CASE

SENSATIONAL ARREST IN EASTON

They went to the mayor's office first, and the mayor was delighted to see them.

"Max. Allison. You did it. You caught the killer and held off the press."

"Well, held them off of you, at any rate," said Max. "Allison wasn't so lucky. They've been hounding her for over a week."

"But you handled it beautifully," said the mayor. "Oh, by the way. With all the publicity, I thought it best to store the painting in the vault of the bank."

Max nodded. "Good idea. We don't want it stolen twice."

"I've had a busy morning," the mayor said, excitedly. "I've had calls from Governor Ritchie, the State Department, and the French Ambassador. They're standing in line to thank us."

"Should come in handy next election," Max observed.

"Now the State Department wants to have a fancy ceremony here next week to turn the painting over to the

French, but Governor Ritchie wants to display it at the Baltimore Museum of Art for a month first. The Smithsonian wants it for a while also, but that's not up to me. They'll all have to work it out."

"So what about Glenn Stilwell," Max asked. "Is he going to be charged?"

The mayor looked relieved. "Probably not. The French don't want to publicize the fact that they didn't know what happened to their own painting, or that an American saved it, and the State Department doesn't want a lot a publicity about American diplomats stealing French artworks. They've seized on Stilwell's letter to his attorney to assure themselves his intentions were noble. So it looks like Glenn Stilwell emerges as something of a folk hero."

"Sort of like the monks preserving manuscripts during the dark ages, I suppose," Allison remarked. "So are we invited to this ceremony?"

"Well, with all the dignitaries, there won't be room for you on the dais," said the mayor, "but you can certainly come."

"Thanks a bunch," said Allison.

The door to the office suddenly opened and the mayor's assistant came in with what looked like a large poster.

"Sorry to interrupt, but you said you wanted to see this as soon as we got it. Take a look."

He held up the poster, revealing it to consist of a large photograph of the *Smiling Angel of Reims*, proudly flanked by the mayor on one side and Chief Vickers on the other.

"It would appear there's a new masterpiece in town," said Max dryly, "the smiling mayor of Easton."

'Well, it's just for the benefit of the newspapers of course," said the mayor.

"Of course," said Max.

"So, would you like me to continue with the press briefings?" Allison asked.

"No, no. I'll take it from here," said the mayor. "Good job, both of you. Thanks again."

Back outside, Allison shook her head. "I don't mind getting the heave ho, Max, but you should have gotten a bit more credit. After all, they arrested the wrong man until you untangled things."

"All in a day's work, my love. Besides, I have a feeling Bob Avery's article will more than make up for any shortcomings in credit from the mayor. Say, isn't that Chip Carswell?"

"Hey Max. Hey Allison," said Chip, catching up to them. "So how did you figure it all out?"

"It was a joint effort," said Max.

"Yeah; Chief Vickers stood back and you cleaned up the joint," said Chip. "Well, my article will talk about what you did even if you don't want to tell me."

"Good old Chip," said Allison. "Of course Bob Avery is interviewing us for a human interest article in the brown section of the Sunday Sun."

Chip looked startled. "What? Say, that's a great idea. When are you meeting him?"

"In about an hour."

"Great. That'll give me time to interview you for *my* article. Come on; I'll buy you both a coffee."

As they started walking down the street, Max whispered to Allison. "I don't think the mayor will be too happy when he sees these articles about how marvelous we are. They're liable to rain on his parade. He was counting on us staying out of sight so he could take the bows."

Allison shrugged. "Maybe next time he'll give you more credit. Now, if I can just find Al White..."

"Al White from the Washington Post?" Max asked.

"Well, I wouldn't want him to feel left out, in case he wants to do an article on us as well."

Max shook his head. "You know, I think you really will be one heck of a mother. You have a strong instinct to look out for people you care about. You're the Smiling Angel of the Eastern Shore."

She stopped and looked at him. "Not yet, Max...but I will be."


The End

Notes

**The Laundryman Murder**- Death on the Eastern Shore is fiction, but is based on several real crimes. In March of 1929, Isidor Fink was found shot to death in his laundry in a residential/office building at 132nd Street near Fifth Avenue in New York City. Neighbors heard screams, but no shots. The door was bolted from the inside and the only access was by a small transom window. No weapon was found, and the presence of powder burns indicated that Fink was not shot from the transom. The cash register was not touched and Fink still had money in his pockets. The case was never solved.

**Reims Cathedral and the Smiling Angel**- The lost painting in the story is based on the real Smiling Angel of Reims, a stone sculpture on the central portal of the cathedral of Notre Dame de Reims in Reims, France. Reims Cathedral is where the kings of France were crowned, including Charles VII, accompanied by Joan of Arc. The cathedral was heavily damaged by German artillery in World War I. On one such shelling, a fire started and caused the head of the smiling angel to fall and break, causing outrage in France at the time. After the war, the statue was restored in 1926, the time Death across the Chesapeake takes place.

**Art theft and art forgery**- Theft of art treasures was widespread during both world wars, but peaked in World War II when the Nazi government systematically looted the rest of Europe. Many of these treasures have never been recovered. At the same time, there has been a thriving market in both stolen art, and in art forgeries. The most famous stolen art was the 1911 theft of the Mona Lisa referred to in the story. The painting was stolen by a museum employee, Vincenzo Peruggia, an Italian who said he wished to restore it to Italy. (Ironically the painting was never stolen from Italy in the first place, but was sold to French King Francois I.) Peruggia kept the painting hidden in his rooms for two years. One account indicates that Peruggia had friends that were forgers and who stood to gain by selling copies once the original was stolen. Peruggia was caught when he grew impatient and tried to sell the Mona Lisa to the Uffizi Gallery in Italy. The idea that a stolen or missing painting would make forgeries more valuable is the basis for Death on the Eastern Shore.

**The Stilwells, the Stilwell Building and Casa Leone**- The Stilwells are based on a real life eccentric wealthy couple who came to live near St Michaels, Maryland in the 1920s. They built a mysterious and well-guarded mansion on the water, converted an old hotel in Easton into an office building, and named it after themselves, just as in the story. They were known for erratic and extravagant behavior, including raising Irish Wolfhounds, and employing armed guards. The mansion still stands, but the name of the people and the location of the mansion have been changed to protect the privacy of the present residents.

**The Norge Expedition**- In 1926, an expedition set off from Norway in the Italian airship Norge in an attempt to fly over the North Pole. Norwegian explorer

Roald Amundsen had organized the expedition and it was acclaimed as the first overflight of the North Pole. The airship encountered high wind and was not able to land at Nome Alaska as planned, but landed elsewhere in Alaska. Years later, when Amundsen's flight diary was examined, some critics claimed the navigational data was fraudulent. In addition, Amundsen and the Italian designer and pilot argued about who should get the most credit. Mussolini got into the act, sending the Italians on a U.S. speaking tour, further aggravating the Norwegians.

**The voyage of the Deutschland-** In 1916, the German submarine Deutschland made a goodwill visit to America, a visit that included Baltimore. The Deutschland was a privately built submarine designed to carry cargo through the British blockade of Germany. Her visit to Baltimore was a great success. The crewmen were treated as celebrities and taken to dinner. The Deutschland stayed about a month before returning to Germany. The submarine made other journeys running cargos to and from Germany, and found time to sink a great deal of Allied shipping with her deck gun. Although nearly sunk several times, the Deutschland survived the war and was broken up for scrap.

One of the unintended effects of the Deutschland's voyage to Baltimore, came about years later, when Maryland was planning the construction of the first Chesapeake Bay Bridge. Remembering the sight of a German submarine cruising up and down the bay, Baltimore shipping interests argued for a tunnel because of the possibility of an enemy collapsing the bridge across the main ship channel. Although a bridge was built, tunnels were used crossing the two ship channels at the mouth of the bay.

**Rumrunning syndicates**- During the early days of Prohibition, enforcement was lax and ineffective, so pretty much anyone with a still or a boat could go into business for himself around the Chesapeake Bay. By 1926, when the story takes place, however, things had tightened up. Better surveillance, better radio communications, more enforcement resources made running liquor across the bay in a workboat very risky. The only way to avoid being intercepted was to consolidate the trips with a large, specially designed speedboat, a strategy far beyond the resources of individuals. As a result, the rumrunners pooled their resources. Rumrunning went from being controlled by small players to organized crime syndicates. No one else had the money, the lawyers, or the political connections to deal with the risks involved.

**University of Maryland and Goucher College**- When Max and Allison refer to Max's schooling in most of the Hurlock stories, they say he attended the University of Maryland, but when Max entered in 1913, it was the Maryland Agricultural College, a land grant college dedicated to agriculture and technical subjects. In 1916, when Max met Allison, the school was renamed the Maryland State College, and finally became the University of Maryland in 1920, after Max had graduated.

Allison attended Goucher College, now located in Towson, Maryland, but at the time Allison attended, Goucher College was in downtown Baltimore on 23rd

Street. The area is now an historic district. Goucher College was originally the Women's College of Baltimore City, but was renamed in 1910.

---

Other adventures of Max and Allison Hurlock

Death of a Flapper
How did the most popular girl in town and her ex-fiancée end up dead and half-dressed in her locked bedroom? A distraught parent begs Max Hurlock to find the truth, but another murder occurs and the suspicious local police arrest Max for the crime!

*"...fun and interesting, crammed with tidbits of historical information that gives it flavor and captures 1922 and early years of the Roaring 20s with real gusto."* Amazon Review

Death on a Golden Isle
Death crashes the party at an exclusive island club for millionaires when a member is poisoned at the club dance. All eyes turn to his new wife and she turns to Max Hurlock to crack the case. But how do you pry secrets out of the most powerful men in America?

*"...a delightful visit to an era, long past, with suspicions, secrets and clues woven through summer mansions, the exclusive club, and into shadowy hunting grounds."* Amazon Review

## Death at the Lighthouse

It's lights out on the Chesapeake Bay when a lighthouse keeper is murdered. Was it local rumrunners, a jealous husband, or something even more sinister? Max and Allison Hurlock must get to the bottom of a case involving rumrunners, jealous husbands, watermen, spiritualists, a corrupt federal agent, and a certain well-known magician.

*"Mark me down as a super-fan of John Reisinger. I predict that every lover of an exciting tale told well will agree."* Anne Stinson, Tidewater Times Book Review

## Death and the Blind Tiger

Ellsworth Connelly seemed to have it all. Operating out of his opulent bachelor townhome, Connelly left a string of jilted women, outraged husbands, and resentful business partners in his wake. Was it any wonder he was found in his own parlor shot through the head? To exonerate his client, Max must deal with the local police, bootleggers, and assorted New York characters such as Duke Ellington, while Allison goes to the Algonquin round table to match wits with Dorothy Parker. Their only clue is a blindfolded ceramic tiger...sent by the dead man!

*(Gold Medal winner in Mystery category- 2104 Global E-Book Awards)*

*"...takes the reader from the elegant homes of wealthy New Yorkers to the seamier side of a city living under Prohibition, and weaves the threads of that event through the story."* Amazon Review

### Death in Unlikely Places

The Florida real estate boom is falling apart and someone is killing the biggest real estate developers in spectacular and impossible ways. One is stabbed in his locked office, apparently while shooting at the killer; one is killed while in a boat on a lake in view of a marina; one is killed in an elevator between floors; one is found draped over a tree branch 15 feet in the air; and one is shot while alone in a private gallery whose only door is in constant view of dozens of witnesses. The killer is so elusive, he is being called The Invisible Man, and a famous aviation pioneer calls on Max Hurlock to get to the bottom of it. Can Max Hurlock make sense of these mysterious events? More to the point, can he stop them? In this fifth Max Hurlock mystery, enter the world of Florida in the Roaring 20s and meet real estate barons, tin can tourists, crackers, bootleggers, and even a Voodoo priestess. As Allison would say "St Michaels was never like this."

*"I would definitely recommend this book to anyone who enjoys mystery and desires to brush up on history at the same time."* Amazon Review

Books by John Reisinger

The Max Hurlock Roaring 20s Mysteries
Death of a Flapper
Death on a Golden Isle
Death at the Lighthouse
Death and the Blind Tiger
Death in Unlikely Places
Death across the Chesapeake

Historical novels
Flanagan and the Crown of Mexico
Nassau
Evasive Action
The Confessions of Gonzalo Guererro

Biography
Master Detective: The Life and Crimes of Ellis Parker, America's Real-life Sherlock Holmes

Children's
The Duckworth Chronicles
The Duckworth Papers
The Duckworth Dossier
Duckworth Redux

www.johnreisinger.com

About the author

John Reisinger lives on Maryland's Eastern Shore, and is the author of Master Detective, the true story of detective Ellis Parker and his controversial involvement in the Lindbergh kidnapping investigation.

He also writes the Max Hurlock Roaring 20s Mysteries, based on real crimes of that era, as well as of several historical novels, including Nassau, Evasive Action, Flanagan and the Crown of Mexico, and The Confessions of Gonzalo Guererro.

John has appeared as a panelist or solo presenter at Deadly Ink, Malice Domestic, New England Crime Bake and Bouchercon conferences. Several of his presentations have been broadcast on local television and radio. John has also appeared on the TV series Mysteries at the Museum in a segment based on Master Detective.

His website is http://www.johnreisinger.com, and his blog is http://johnreisinger/wordpress.com

www.ingramcontent.com/pod-product-compliance
Lightning Source LLC
Chambersburg PA
CBHW020048180626
46812CB00006B/2233